GAMES LOVERS PLAY

Connie Morgan works in the haberdashery department of a large Southampton store, and is in love with her married boss. But everything changes when she's swept off her feet by dashing young car mechanic Sam. Having fallen head over heels for Sam, Connie is anxious to end her adulterous affair with John Baker. But John isn't going to let her go that easily, and Connie knows that if Sam ever finds out about her relationship with a married man, he will end everything, dashing all her dreams. So Connie decides to keep quiet – but she is playing a dangerous game...

GAMES LOVERS PLAY

GAMES LOVERS PLAY

by

June Tate

Magna Large Print Books
Long Preston, North Yorkshire,
BD23 4ND, England.

British Library Cataloguing in Publication Data.

Tate, June
  Games lovers play.

  A catalogue record of this book is
  available from the British Library

  ISBN   978-0-7505-4090-2

First published in Great Britain in 2013 by
Severn House Publishers Ltd.

Copyright © 2013 by June Tate

Cover illustration © Malgorzata Maj by arrangement with
Arcangel Images

The moral right of the author has been asserted

Published in Large Print 2015 by arrangement with
Severn House Publishers Ltd.

Magna Large Print is an imprint of Library Magna Books Ltd.

Printed and bound in Great Britain by
T.J. (International) Ltd., Cornwall, PL28 8RW

With love to Ann Jones and her delightful family and remembering Pat with great affection.

Acknowledgements

With thanks to Rachel Simpson Hutchens for her meticulous copy-editing and as always my love to my two daughters, Beverley and Maxine.

One

March, 1955

Madge Morgan looked disparagingly at Connie, her granddaughter. 'You and your flighty ways! It'll all end in tears – you'll see.'

'For goodness' sake, Nan, I'm nineteen, not a child any longer. I'm perfectly old enough to know what I'm doing!' And she flounced out of the room, slamming the front door behind her as she left the house.

'Miserable old bat!' she muttered as she walked down the road. Her grandmother had moved in with the family after her husband died and had cast a cloud of enmity over the household ever since. She was full of doom and gloom, giving her opinions on everything and interfering – or trying to.

'Well, she's not ruining *my* life,' Connie vowed. Life was to be lived. She wasn't going to grow old and embittered like the old girl. Not her! She was going to have a good time if it killed her!

She caught the bus, alighting at the Civic Centre which was near to Tyrell and Greens, the large prestigious department store in Above Bar, where she worked in the haberdashery department. Hanging her coat in the staff room, she hurried to her counter ready for the first customer.

John Baker, the floor manager, walked over to her. 'Good morning, Connie, you look nice.'

'Thank you, Mr Baker,' she said, trying to look demure. Then she smiled softly and in a very low voice said, 'You look good enough to eat!'

He tried to keep a straight face as Betty, her friend and workmate, joined them.

'Well, girls, let's hope we have a profitable day today,' he said as he walked away.

'Your boyfriend checking up on you, is he?' Betty asked sarcastically.

'He's not my boyfriend!' Connie snapped back at her.

'Bloody right he isn't. The man has a wife and kiddie. You should remember that. Oh Connie, I'm only worried about you. When a married man comes sniffing round a young girl, he's after only one thing.'

'He's only ever kissed me, that's all.' She didn't tell her friend of the intimate caresses she'd shared with him, in a dark corner of the town, when they had met occasionally for a quiet drink. John Baker was fourteen years her senior, but to Connie he was a man of enviable sophistication. The way he dressed, his carriage, his knowledge – and when he kissed her, he stirred unexpected longings in her.

14

She knew he wanted her, he'd told her often enough. He'd said that he wasn't happy with his wife, but as they had a child he couldn't leave her, he had a duty to stay and bring up their daughter. So far, she'd managed to fend off his more amorous advances, but she knew it was just a matter of time, and she'd decided that she would eventually lose her virginity to him.

'How about going to the Guildhall tonight?' asked Betty. 'It's the best night of the week there. All the people who can really dance turn out. What do you say?'

'Yes, I'd love to!' It was just what she needed. She was getting bored. Nothing exciting was happening, and how much longer could she wait for Mr Baker?

That evening, Connie waited outside the Guildhall for her friend Betty. They both loved to dance, and every ballroom was full of eager young men, out for a good time. There were very few wallflowers these days, and she was never without a partner. Connie was an attractive girl with short, naturally curly hair and wide green eyes. There was an exuberance about her personality that was charming.

'Connie!'

She turned at the sound of her name and grinned when she saw her friend running towards her. Betty was renowned for being late. Connie sometimes teased her, saying she would be late for her own wedding. But Betty would just laugh and say that would be the one time in her life when she'd be early in case the groom changed his mind!

After leaving their coats in the cloakroom, the girls walked upstairs to the ballroom. The band was playing Cole Porter's 'Night and Day'.

'Oh, I love this song,' said Connie. 'It's so romantic.' She looked quickly around the room. Apart from the boys in civvies, there were several British servicemen in various uniforms. This pleased Connie because they were usually good dancers and good company.

'Come on,' said Connie and dragged her friend to the edge of the floor where they could pick out the best of the dancers. 'Keep clear of that one,' she said, pointing out a soldier. 'He's got two left feet. He'll be standing on yours more than his own. Look … see what I mean?'

The soldier's partner winced as he stepped on her toes.

'If that were me,' Betty remarked, 'I'd make my excuses now and leave. Last week some twit literally walked me round the room. After that I swore to myself I'd never put up with another bad dancer, it wastes too much time.'

The music stopped, and they watched the

girl in question limp off the floor.

'There you are! Her night is ruined,' Betty said angrily. 'Silly girl.'

As the band started to play a quickstep, a young man sauntered over to Connie. 'Can you jive?' he asked, grinning broadly.

'Of course I can!'

He held out his hand. 'Then let's do it.'

He whirled her round the floor, spinning her in time to the music. Her layered petticoat swished this way and that until the number finished.

He looked at her with some admiration. 'You were good,' he said. 'You deserve a drink, I'm thirsty after that. What's your name, by the way?'

'Connie.'

'Well, hello, Connie, I'm Sam. Come on.'

He was good company, and he made her laugh. She learned that he was a car mechanic and at weekends he raced old cars at various rallies around the county. To Connie it sounded exciting.

'I'm racing next Sunday,' he said. 'Why don't you come with me?'

She thought, why not? It was just the change she needed at this moment. 'I'd love to,' she told him.

They spent the rest of the evening dancing together, and when the last waltz was played he held her close. 'Can I walk you home, Connie? Then I'll know where to pick you up on Sunday.'

She agreed, and they left the Guildhall together after she'd found her friend Betty, who was also being taken home by a man she'd met.

'We'll swop stories tomorrow,' Betty said with a chuckle.

Sam held her hand as they walked through the park and up Hill Lane to Archers Road. He was different from John Baker in every way. He was younger, full of youthful enthusiasm, and Connie felt at ease with him as they talked and she learned of his ambition.

'One day, Connie, I'll specialize in racing cars. I like building engines, getting them ready for the track. It's a specialized job, and I'm good at it.'

She liked his air of confidence, his self belief, his honesty. There was no hidden agenda here, as far as she could tell. She wondered just what Sam would think of her if he knew of her liaison with a married man. She thought he would be disappointed.

They stopped outside her house, and he walked her up the side path. 'Don't want your old man opening the door on us, do we?' He took her into his arms and kissed her.

He was strong and held her tightly as his mouth explored hers. She kissed him back, surprised to discover how experienced he seemed to be, and she wondered how many girls he had bedded and then felt guilty at such thoughts. But he didn't attempt to touch her other than to hold her, and for this she was relieved. It would have spoiled the evening.

He brushed a stray hair from her face. 'I'm so pleased we met, Connie, and I look forward to Sunday. I'll pick you up at nine o'clock.' He waited until she'd opened the door and stepped inside and then with a wave, he left.

As she walked upstairs to her room, she smiled. There, Mr Baker, she thought, you're not the only pebble on the beach by a long chalk!

Sam was very punctual and arrived at Connie's door at nine o'clock on Sunday morning. When she opened it she was surprised to see a racing car outside painted a bright red with a white circle with a number nine in the middle.

Seeing her dismay, Sam grinned. 'This is Gracie, my racer. Get in!'

As she did so she saw the curtain of the front room twitch and smiled to herself. She knew it would be her grandmother, who could never keep her nose out of other people's business. Well, this would really give her something to think about!

Sam started the engine, which seemed to roar as he put his foot on the accelerator, and drove away. As they journeyed through the town, people stopped and stared at the vehicle as it passed, and Connie felt privileged to be sitting beside the driver. They headed for the New Forest, and Connie sat back and admired the view. Sam didn't say a great deal other than to ask her if she was all right, as he was concentrating on the traffic.

He eventually pulled off the road and wound his way through the numerous parked cars and on to a piece of land beside a racetrack. Connie was amazed at the scene before her, having been unaware that such a place existed. Various makes of racing cars were being scrutinized by officials, engines being attended to by their drivers. There was a noisy buzz about the place, and she felt her excitement quicken.

She and Sam got out of the car, and he put on a pair of racing overalls. He was immediately surrounded by onlookers and two men who quickly lifted the bonnet of the car to inspect the engine. Sam hurriedly introduced her to his friends. They muttered a quick hello before burying their heads beneath the bonnet.

Eventually, the vehicle was deemed to be in order and the first race began. Sam took her to the side of the track to explain what was going on.

'There are several heats, Connie, and the winners of each heat race against each other in the final one.' He put an arm around her as he pointed out the tactics of the drivers, who seemed to her to be driving like mad men.

'They look as if they're trying to push each other off the track!' she exclaimed.

He laughed. 'They are! It's the quick and the dead out there, Connie.'

She was horrified as one car tipped over on its side, at speed, and she clutched hold of him in fear.

'Don't worry,' he said. 'When you're racing you're well strapped in, and we wear helmets to protect our heads.' They watched the next two heats and then Sam said, 'I have to leave you now, Connie. I'm racing in this one.'

She cast a worried glance in his direction.

'Tom!' he called to one of his friends. 'Take care of Connie, will you? Try and assure her that I'm not facing certain death.' He kissed her on the cheek. 'Don't worry. I'll be fine and I'm going to win!'

As she watched him walk towards his car, he strapped a helmet on to his head. Then he climbed into the vehicle, started the engine and with a wave drove on to the track and made his way to the starting line.

His friend Tom stood beside her. 'Don't you worry about Sam,' he told her, 'he's one of the best drivers around. That boy's got talent. He could go a long way in this sport. Honestly. Watch and learn!'

With her heart thumping, Connie felt tense as she watched for the starting flag. The sound of revving engines was deafening, and the smell of petrol fumes filled the air. Then the flag dropped and they were off!

Connie lost count of the number of laps around the circuit; her gaze was glued to Sam and his car. She held her breath as he weaved in and out, moving up the field. Several cars came to grief and withdrew from the race, after being shunted off the track by oncoming fast-moving vehicles! She cried out as another driver purposely edged his car towards Sam, but with clever steering he moved quickly away from the danger.

She was outraged. Turning to Tom she said, 'Did you see what that driver tried to do? He was trying to drive Sam off the track. That's dangerous!'

He laughed. 'It's all part of the game, but as you saw, Sam was ready for him. He has a nose for such things. It takes a clever driver to better him. Don't worry!'

'But that's playing dirty!' she protested.

'This is a dirty game, Connie, on and off the track.'

She wondered just what he meant, but the excitement of the race made her forget his strange remark. Exhausted but pepped up by adrenalin and excitement she cheered as Sam eventually drove over the winning line into first place.

Tom grinned at her. 'What did I tell you?' he said.

Her hand clasped her chest. 'I can hardly breathe,' she gasped.

'You'd better get used to all this if you're going to keep seeing Sam. This is his life.'

They waited for Sam to drive off the track and park his car. He alighted and took off his helmet and goggles, grinning broadly at her.

'There you are, Connie. I told you I was going to win!'

She flung her arms around him in her excitement. 'I nearly died with worry!' she blurted out, then realizing what she'd done she let go and stepped back, blushing with embarrassment.

He reached for her hand. 'Don't go away, I liked that.' And he leaned forward and kissed her soundly. 'Winner takes all,' he said as he released her.

His friends looked on with amusement.

The day was the most thrilling of her life she decided. True to his word, Sam won the final race, and as he stood on the podium to take the trophy, she was thrilled to be with him. As he stepped down he searched her out and gave her a quick smile and a wink, then he went into the gents to wash the grime from the track off his face and remove his overalls and change into a clean shirt he'd brought with him.

Walking back to Connie, he said, 'The boys and I always go for a beer after a race, then we can go to dinner. All right with you?'

'Of course,' she said. 'Now I'm ready for anything.'

The men gathered in a nearby pub and over a couple of pints ran over the details of the race together, and afterwards they talked about Stirling Moss, the first Briton to win the Mille Miglia road race in Italy, which to Connie meant nothing. She listened with great interest, nevertheless. This was a new world to her and one that she found thrilling.

When eventually the men left, they said goodbye to Connie, and Tom said, 'See you again, Connie. Next time you'll know what to expect.'

She fervently hoped there would be a next time because she'd never had so much fun and Sam was quite different from anyone she'd ever met. Certainly from John Baker. Suddenly, he didn't seem quite so important any more.

They drove back to Southampton and to the Cowherds Hotel on the edge of the Common – an area of parkland with lakes, which had lots of paths so the public could enjoy the well-tended shrubs and greenery.

Sam, it appeared, was well-known by the staff. Several enquired as to how the race went and didn't seem at all surprised that he was the winner. The head waiter himself tended to their needs after seating them at a table.

Sam handed Connie a menu. 'I don't know about you, but I'm starving!' he said.

She realized that she was too, now that she'd calmed down. They ordered hors d'oeuvres, followed by duck, and meringue with strawberries as dessert, to be washed down with a good bottle of wine. She was surprised as to how knowledgeable he was about the wine list. She hadn't imagined that he would be, but how stupid to jump to such a conclusion! After all, she didn't know anything about him, but after dining with John on the odd occasion she had taken it for granted only men of a certain age would know such things.

As they waited for their first course, sipping the wine that had been poured, Sam gazed at Connie and asked, 'Did you enjoy yourself today?'

Her eyes shone as she showed her pleasure. 'Oh, Sam, of course I did. It was so exciting! I had no idea what was going to happen. When you told me you raced cars, I had no idea what it entailed.'

'Well, not all women are interested in the sport, you know. I didn't want to put you off.'

She looked at him in amazement. 'Put me off? I've never had such a marvellous time in my whole life!'

He burst out laughing. 'Your whole life? All what – nineteen years, I would say?'

'Yes, well,' she muttered. 'Even so, it was wonderful.'

Reaching across the table for her hand, he said, 'I'm so pleased, because I want to see you again. But I have to warn you, you take me *and* the racing. Don't be in any doubt. If you go out with me, a lot of my time is spent with my car and others I'm building. Do you mind?'

'Not at all,' she said firmly.

After dinner, he drove her away from the Cowherds and parked in a quiet side road off the common. He turned off the engine and took her into his arms, kissing her with fervour.

'I'm so happy you were there today. It was lovely to have someone cheering for me in my corner.'

'Oh, Sam, you had lots of people cheering for you as well as me.'

He stroked her cheek. 'I know, but you were someone special, and I liked that. Would you like to come and see a film with me on Thursday? I'm sorry but I'm not free until then.'

'I'd love to,' she said.

'I'll meet you outside the Forum at six thirty and we can decide which film to see.'

'That'll be fine,' she said.

He took her into his arms again and kissed her. 'Until then, sweet Connie. Now I'd better get you home.'

When they reached their destination, she climbed out of the car and waved Sam goodbye. She felt sure the whole neighbourhood heard the roar of his motor as he drove away.

She opened the front door and entered. No doubt she would face a third degree from Madge. Well, today she didn't care. She'd had such a good time that no one could spoil it for her!

Her parents, George and Dorothy, were sitting reading the local paper, and Madge, in her dressing gown, hair in curlers beneath a pink hairnet, was drinking cocoa. She couldn't wait to question her granddaughter.

'So where have you been all day then?' She didn't wait for an answer. 'I saw you take off in that car... The noise it made would have woken the dead!'

Her mother looked up from the paper. 'So tell us all about it, Connie. Your grandmother was full of it!'

'Yes, I bet she nearly fell over herself to give you all the details,' Connie retorted.

'That'll do, Connie!' her father said sharply.

'I've been out in the New Forest with Sam, who's a racing driver! There's a track out there where they race. Oh, it was so exciting ... and he won!' she announced with great pride.

'Where did you meet this young man?' her father asked.

'At the Guildhall, and he asked me out.'

'So you don't know anything about him!' snapped Madge.

'Not as yet, Nan, but I intend to. I'm going to the pictures with him on Thursday.' She walked towards the stairs. 'I'm tired so I'm off to bed. Goodnight.' And she left before she could be questioned further.

As she undressed she relived the excitement of the day and again wondered about Tom's remark. She could see how the track racing could be dirty, but off the track too? Whatever could he mean? She would ask Sam when she saw him next.

The following morning, Monday, she regaled Betty with all the details of her day. Her friend listened avidly. 'Bloody hell, Connie, how exciting! Do you like him, honestly?'

'Yes, he's really nice. He introduced me to his friends too, and they seemed a nice bunch.'

'Is he single?' Betty looked at her with curiosity. 'You don't want to get mixed up with another married bloke!'

'I don't think he's married,' Connie said. 'From the way he spoke he's married to car racing. He told me I'd have to accept that if I wanted to go out with him again.'

Betty chuckled. 'Well, at least a car isn't as

dangerous as a wife!'

'You wouldn't think that if you saw what happened on the racetrack. It was very hairy at times, I can tell you!'

On Thursday evening, Connie sat with Sam in the cinema, where he bought her chocolates and sat with his arm around her during the performance of *Marty,* starring Ernest Borgnine, and after took her for a drink. It was in the bar as they sat together that Connie broached the subject that had been in the back of her mind.

'Tom told me that car racing was a dirty business. What did he mean?'

He raised his eyebrows in surprise. 'Did he? Well, Connie, there's a lot of money to be won for the race winners in some competitions and some of the teams aren't too fussy about how they accomplish that goal. But you shouldn't worry your head about such things.'

Connie, realizing that was the end of the conversation as far as he was concerned, remained silent.

'I'd love to see you over the weekend, Connie, but I'll be working on a car ... unless you'd like to come to the garage on Sunday? I'll have some sandwiches and a flask of tea we could share.'

'I'd love to come,' she said. 'I'm really interested to see what you do.'

He seemed very pleased at her response. 'If you are really interested, perhaps when I've got a bit of free time I'll teach you to drive. Then you'll understand what it feels like behind a wheel of a car... But no racing for you, understand? It's far too dangerous!'

She was speechless with delight.

Two

Just before noon on Sunday morning, Connie made her way to the Chapel area of Southampton. It had always been a poorer area of the town and had been badly bombed during the Blitz in 1940, when much of Southampton had been destroyed. Indeed, apart from clearing away the debris, some places were still just a shell. The streets had an air of despair and neglect. Nevertheless, the few houses that remained sported net curtains at the windows and one or two had tried to make some semblance of a garden in the very small area in front. But two tubs of geraniums and a patch of weed-filled grass didn't make much of an improvement.

Connie found the garage easily enough. The doors were wide open, a wireless blared out, and there was much banging and crashing from within. She stepped inside and looked around. On one wall were shelves filled with boxes, their contents marked on the outside. In the centre was a vehicle, and on the ground were several car parts, waiting to be fitted. The car bonnet was up, and two bodies were bent over, working on the engine, oblivious to anything else. Connie stood, wondering what to do, when a voice behind her made her turn.

'Hello, Connie! Come to give us a hand then?' It was Tom.

She laughed. 'I wouldn't know where to begin,' she said.

'Well, you could help me make the tea for those two.' He nodded towards the car. 'It's the only thing that will get them out.' He walked over to the car and prodded one of the bodies. 'Hey, Sam! Your girlfriend's here!'

Sam uncurled himself and stood up. His face was streaked with oil, but even so when he smiled at Connie she felt her heart beat a little faster.

'There you are! I wondered what time you'd come.' He kissed her gingerly on the cheek. 'Sorry, but this is a pretty messy job, as you can see.' He took a rag and wiped his hands. 'Where's that bloody tea then, Tom?'

His mate grinned at him. 'Just you be patient, my lad, it's coming up. Here, Connie, give these cups a rinse, will you?' He handed her three cups and pointed to a sink she'd not seen.

She willingly did as she was asked, and when she'd finished Sam and the other man, Harry, whom she'd hastily been introduced to at the race meeting, washed their hands.

'That's better,' said Sam, 'now we can stop for lunch.'

'I've brought you some sandwiches,' she told him. 'Egg and cress. I hope that will be all right?'

'You beauty!' Sam cried and hugged her. 'That's really nice of you.'

'Yes, you can come again,' Tom said with a laugh, and Harry beamed his approval.

They sat on upturned boxes, and with her sandwiches, plus the ones the boys had brought with them, they sat down to a veritable feast.

Part-way through lunch the sound of a motorcycle engine made the men stop eating and watch the garage entrance. Connie immediately felt the atmosphere change. There was an air of tension, and she wondered why. None of the men spoke, they just watched as the sound grew nearer. A motorcyclist drew up outside and gazed in, but when he saw the men staring at him, he drove away. She looked over at Sam and saw his eyes narrow and his lips purse as he looked at his friends. But no one said anything, and although she was filled with curiosity, she kept quiet.

As they finished eating and drank the tea, Sam explained that the vehicle in the garage was a different racing car he was working on for forthcoming races.

'It's more powerful than Gracie, my other

one. I'm hoping to clear the board with it,' he said.

Tom chimed in. 'He should be able to do so too ... as long as no one interferes.'

Sam looked at him and frowned. Tom didn't say any more.

'You'll be my lucky mascot,' said Sam and leaned over and kissed her cheek.

'Oh my word,' she said quickly. 'What if something goes wrong? You'll blame me!'

His look of affection dispelled her fears. 'I'd never do that, Connie. Any race has its chance of things going wrong. Things that happen unexpectedly – however carefully you've planned a race – can change everything. It's all part and parcel of the game.'

'Don't you worry about Sam,' said Tom. 'He's a great driver; I told you so on Sunday.'

'Did he?' Sam asked, looking really pleased with the compliment.

'Yes, he did.'

'And of course he's right,' Harry said. 'Are you going to stick around, Connie, and see if Tom's right?'

With eyes sparkling, she said, 'I certainly am! I wouldn't miss it for the world.'

'That's my girl! We'll have to get you a pair of team overalls, I can see.'

She was delighted. But as she walked home alone after, she wondered just what was going on, because something certainly was. The motorcyclist had come for a purpose. But what?

Sam was working away the following week, and Connie felt restless, and when John Baker walked over to her counter, she greeted him with a smile.

Quietly, he said, 'My wife's taking our daughter away for the weekend to stay with her mother.'

Connie felt her heart thumping as she waited to hear what was coming next.

'I thought we could go down to Bournemouth on Saturday night after work, book into a hotel, have dinner somewhere nice and come back on Sunday. What do you think?'

She felt a moment of excitement – then panic. Here was the opportunity she'd been waiting for, but now it was a reality she felt scared. So far during their clandestine meetings, she'd kept him at bay, teasing him, but in a hotel room she'd be expected to have sex with him.

Sensing her dilemma, he gazed into her eyes and said softly, 'I can't wait to hold you in my arms without worrying about being seen. I'll take good care of you, Connie. I promise you'll enjoy it as much as I will.' He waited.

She stood looking at him, wondering what to do. This man had such a hold over her that she found it hard to resist his invitation. Then he smiled at her, and she was lost. Taking a deep breath, she said, 'I'd love to.'

There was a look of triumph in his eyes. 'That's wonderful. Bring a case with your things on Saturday, and after we close go to the station, I'll meet you there.'

She watched him walk away, now nervous but also thrilled about the prospect of the weekend ahead.

Betty sidled up to her. 'What was all that about then?'

'Nothing, just telling me about some stock due in tomorrow,' she said, and she moved away.

Betty frowned. Connie was lying, she was sure. She didn't trust John Baker one little bit, and she was concerned for her friend, but business was brisk and she didn't have time to question Connie further. By the time she'd finished and collected her things from the staff room, Connie had already left the building.

During the following days, Connie fended off any further questions from Betty, and as Saturday loomed, she began to wish she'd refused to go to Bournemouth – yet at the same time, as she tried to sleep at night, she couldn't help trying to visualize being in bed with John. She had already told her mother she was staying with Betty over the weekend.

This didn't raise any questions, as she'd done so many times in the past. It was a much-needed break from the unwelcome attentions of her grandmother, who loudly voiced her concerns about the lack of morals of the young people of today, which were pointedly aimed at Connie.

On Saturday morning, she picked up her small case in which she'd packed the new nightdress and underwear she'd bought during the week and a new pale green dress with a fitted bodice and full skirt. When she'd purchased these things, she couldn't help but be thrilled, feeling she was being really risqué and grown up. She'd leave Southampton a virgin and return a woman! But at the same time, she was worried about her lack of experience in such matters. Would John Baker find her a disappointment? How dreadful that would be.

She hardly saw John during Saturday as the shop was busy, but as she walked towards the staff room at the end of the day, he passed her and winked. She put on her coat and hurried outside before Betty emerged from the ladies' room. She didn't want her friend to see the suitcase. Betty was a bright girl and would immediately guess what was happening.

During the walk to the station, she almost turned back, but curiosity and anticipation overcame her fears and she waited outside the station entrance for the man who was to be her lover. She thought of him as that over and over in her mind. Her lover! How sophisticated that sounded. Whilst she was thinking about this, she saw the man in question striding towards her, smiling as he came closer.

'For one awful moment, I wondered if you'd change your mind,' he confessed.

She lowered her head and looked up at him, coyly. 'Why ever would I do such a thing?' she lied.

Putting his arm around her, he led her into the station. 'I bought the tickets yesterday,' he said. 'We only have ten minutes until the next train, and if there had been a queue, it would have been a rush.'

'You're well prepared,' she observed.

He held her tighter. 'I want you to remember this time we spend together as something very special. I didn't want anything to spoil it.'

They made polite conversation throughout the journey, and when they arrived in Bournemouth they took a taxi to the hotel. Connie watched as he signed the register. *Mr and Mrs J. Baker.* She tucked her left hand into her pocket, aware of the fact she didn't have a wedding ring. Then, taking the key to the room, he led her to the lift. As the doors closed, he took her into his arms and kissed her until she was breathless.

The lift stopped and the doors opened. Looking at the sign upon the wall, he led her along the corridor.

Connie felt the soft carpet beneath her feet as she walked with him, her heart in her mouth as he stopped. He put the key in the door, opened it and led her into the bed-room, closing the door behind him. He took her case from her and led her over to the window.

'Look, darling, we can see the sea from here.' As they both gazed out at the beach and beyond, he slipped the coat from her shoulders and gathered her into his arms from behind, his hands enclosing her breasts as he kissed the back of her neck.

'Oh, Connie, I've longed for this moment,' he whispered as he turned her to face him. His mouth crushed hers, and she felt the tip of his tongue slip into her mouth.

It was as if all her fears evaporated in a second as she returned his kisses.

Before long they lay on the bed together. 'Relax darling,' he said as he began to un-dress her.

He cupped her bare breast in one hand and took the nipple into his mouth. She let out an involuntary moan as his other hand caressed her. A million strange sensations seemed to invade her body, and she writhed beneath his expert hands. Never in her wildest dreams did she think sex could be like this. She no longer was worried about her lack of experience. She was being led by a man who knew his way around the female body and who knew exactly what he was doing, and when eventually he was above her she couldn't wait and begged him to take her.

He chuckled with delight. 'Connie! Oh, Connie, I just knew given the chance you'd be a little ball of fire. You are wonderful!' He thrust himself inside her.

After, he held her in his arms. Connie lay still, confused but elated. Confused because she hadn't been prepared for the sudden pain, but elated as her passion surfaced and she responded to his whispered words as he reached his climax. Yet something was missing. She felt unfulfilled but in her innocence she couldn't understand why.

'Never mind, darling,' he said. 'It takes a while. Next time will be better.'

She wondered how.

Eventually, they dressed and, leaving the room, took the lift and walked out through the reception. Connie looked down, feeling embarrassed, as she passed the desk, wondering if the girl behind it guessed what had just happened. But walking along the front, and stopping at a small restaurant for dinner, soon dispelled such feelings. It was so good to sit at a table with an older man who seemed so sure of himself.

They decided not to have a starter and ordered steak with mushrooms and chips.

John smiled as the waiter left with their order. 'I still can't get used to being able to order meat after so long. Thank God they derationed it last year! I think it was the thing I missed the most.'

She laughed at him. 'That's typical of a man. My dad was always complaining about the same thing. He kept chickens, but in the end he was sick of eating them.'

John flattered her during the meal, boosting her confidence, telling her how lovely she looked, how thrilled he was that at last they were able to be together away from prying eyes, and how happy she made him feel.

'If it wasn't for my daughter, we could spend the rest of our lives together,' he said as he took her hand in his. 'But you do understand my situation, don't you?' he asked. 'After all, I have been honest with you from the beginning.'

What could she say? He'd never led her to believe he could offer anything other than an affair. 'Yes, I do understand,' she replied. But deep down she wished he was free.

That night, when they made love, she had her first orgasm and understood how much better sex could be.

When they arrived back at the station in Southampton, he caught her by the arm. 'I'm off to the gents,' he said. 'We can't be seen leaving together. I'll see you in the shop to-morrow. Here's your ticket.' And he walked away.

His sudden departure took her by surprise, and she felt abandoned and deflated. Miserably, she trudged to the exit and walked up Commercial Road and home.

John Baker emerged from the gents, put his suitcase in the left luggage, went through the exit, bought a platform ticket, re-entered the station, sat on the platform and waited. Half an hour later he got to his feet as the next train steamed in, and when he saw his wife and daughter alight from the train, he walked forward and met them. He kissed his wife, Kay, then picked up his daughter, gave her a hug and said to Kay, 'Hello, darling. Did you have a good time?'

'Yes, thanks, it was lovely to spend time with Mum. She was so pleased to see us. What have you been doing on your own?'

'Not much. I missed you both, the house seemed very empty.'

Connie put her key in the front door and let herself in, and the first person she saw was Madge, her grandmother.

'Well, did you and Betty have a good time together?'

Connie felt the colour flush her cheeks as she answered, 'Yes, thanks, Nan.'

Madge studied her granddaughter. 'Why are you looking so shifty, girl? What have you been up to? Nothing good, I'm sure.'

Connie turned on her. 'Why do you always look for the bad in people? We had a good time doing nothing in particular. We just had fun, but you wouldn't know anything about that would you, Nan?'

'Don't you speak to me like that young lady,' Madge snapped. 'You show me a little respect!'

'I might say the same to you,' Connie retorted and walked out of the room, fuming as she made her way to her bedroom. Putting down her case, she looked at her reflection in the mirror. She didn't look any different. The fact that she'd recently lost her virginity didn't show, thankfully. Lying on her bed, she closed her eyes and relived the days and nights of the past weekend. At least she wouldn't get pregnant, John had taken precautions. She wondered when he'd take her away again. Then she thought of Sam. What would he think of her if he ever found out about her trip to Bournemouth? She didn't think he'd like it, but after all, she told herself, she was free to do as she wanted. She was young and wanted to enjoy life before she got old and miserable like her grandmother. She chuckled softly. No matter what happened to her as she grew old, she'd *never* be like that!

Three

The following day at work, Connie kept looking for John doing his rounds, but when she didn't see him, she casually asked another assistant where he was.

'Oh, he's on holiday for a week,' she told her. 'He said something about going to Devon as his little girl loves playing on the beach there.'

She was shattered. He'd made no mention of a holiday during the time they'd spent together. Now he'd be acting the faithful husband after sharing a bed with her! How could he do such a thing?

'You all right, Connie?' asked Betty as she walked back to the counter. 'You look a little pale.'

'I'm fine,' she answered. But she felt humiliated.

In the workshop of the racing team called the Cheetahs, three men were in a huddle, drinking tea and smoking. There was an air of secrecy about them as they spoke.

'So what *exactly* did you see?' asked one.

The man whose motorcycle helmet rested at his feet said, 'Not much to be honest. As soon as I stopped I saw the three of them and some girl sitting staring out of the door at me. If I'd lingered, they would have come out and asked me what I wanted. They didn't recognize me, fortunately, as I had my visor down.'

'We need to get in somehow and take a good look at the car. Sam Knight is a bloody clever mechanic; he'll know how much he can get out of a souped-up engine. He's a bloody genius when it comes to cars.'

'And behind the wheel,' added another.

'Well, he's not going to bloody well beat me!' snapped Jake Barton, the team driver. 'I'll use whatever means I have to stop him standing on the winner's podium. That's *my* place!'

The other two looked at each other and grimaced. Jake was a sore loser, and Sam Knight was his Achilles heel. Jake was jealous of the other man's success, which he wrongly believed should be his alone. He was a good driver but he was wild and let anger rule his head when driving, which had led to him receiving several warnings during his racing career. The rest of the team worried that this battle with Sam would end up with Jake being banned from racing altogether, and then what would they do?

'Forget about Sam,' one said. 'We have a good car, and if you drive well, you won't have a problem at all.'

Jake flew into a rage. 'What do you mean *if* I drive well? Are you saying I'm a bad driver?'

'For Christ's sake keep your hair on, will you,' said his teammate. 'All I'm saying is if you were to concentrate more on your own car and driving, instead of this insane obsession with Knight, you'd do much better!'

Jake was on his feet in seconds, and before his teammate knew it, Jake had floored him with a punch, then walked out of the garage cursing loudly.

The second man helped his friend to his feet.

Holding his jaw, the victim swore. 'Fucking madman! I'm in two minds to walk away from him and the racing.'

His friend walked over to the sink and ran the cold tap on a cloth, then, after wringing it out, he handed it over. 'Here, put this on your jaw, it'll help with the swelling.'

'One day I'll do for that bastard!' the injured one said. 'I'm sick to death of hearing how good Jake thinks he is and how he should be a winner. Let's be honest, he's no match for Knight, no one is. The man's a genius on the track. He has talent and is a born winner. It's only a matter of luck if he gets a bump that takes him out on the track and enables someone else to take first place. You know it and I know it; unfortunately,

Jake won't accept that fact. Well, sod him! I'm off to the pub for a pint, want to join me?'

They locked up the garage and left.

Connie's mood was lifted when she returned home to find that Sam had written her a letter:

Dear Connie,

I am so sorry to have neglected you this week, but as you know I've been working away. I've missed you, lovely Connie, and to make up for it I'd like to take you out for the day on Sunday. I'll pick you up at eleven in the morning. If this doesn't suit you, leave a message at the garage.

PS. Wear a pair of trousers and a coat and bring a swimsuit and towel.

Lots of love,

Sam xxxx

Connie danced around the room, thrilled to read that he'd missed her, and she couldn't wait to see him.

'You're looking pleased with yourself,' Madge, her grandmother, remarked in her usual sour tone. 'From that boy, is it?'

Connie just raised her eyebrows and tapped her finger on the side of her nose, and left the room.

'Cheeky little bugger!' Madge raged.

'For goodness' sake, what is it now,

Mother?' Dorothy Morgan emerged from the kitchen, wiping her hands on a cloth.

'Your daughter, that's what! She doesn't have an atom of respect for her elders.'

'Perhaps if her elders stopped trying to pry into her affairs, she'd feel differently!'

'Don't you talk to me like that, madam, just remember who I am.'

Dorothy was at the end of her tether. Her mother-in-law had been difficult all day, and she'd had enough. 'As if I could forget! You remind me at least once a day. Now you think on as to who *I* am. I am married to your son and you live in *my* house. I cook for you, do your washing and ironing, clean up behind you, none of which is appreciated, and then you try to make my daughter's life hell as well!'

For once Madge was speechless.

'And what's more, I've just had about enough of you and your moaning interfering ways! Much more of it and I'll be asking your own daughter to house you. You know, the one that hardly ever comes to see you!' She strode out of the room.

The old vixen was deeply shaken by her daughter-in-law's words, and she sat quietly thinking about the tirade that had just been delivered. She knew she was lucky when George, her son, had taken her to live with him and his family, after her husband's death. She had been so relieved because she

49

honestly didn't think she could have coped on her own – not that she had admitted such a thing. She also guessed that Dorothy couldn't have been too happy about the arrangement though. What woman would be? It certainly wasn't an ideal situation. She had to admit she'd been well looked after and she hardly had to lift a finger herself. In fact she'd never offered. But she certainly didn't want to leave and live with Eve, her daughter who'd never had time for her. In fact, if push came to shove, she doubted if Eve would have her! She slowly sipped her now tepid cup of tea. She'd better pull her horns in for a bit, she decided.

On Sunday morning, at eleven o'clock sharp, Connie heard the roar of an engine outside and rushed to the door, calling goodbye over her shoulder. Once outside she realized why Sam had stipulated her wearing trousers. He was sitting astride a large motorbike. He grinned at her and handed her a helmet to wear. Then he instructed her how to sit on the back of the bike.

'Put your arms around my waist,' he told her. 'That way you won't interfere with my driving. You need to relax, and when we corner, lean with me. OK?'

'You won't go too fast, will you?' she asked nervously.

Chuckling, he said, 'Don't worry, Connie.

Do as I ask and you'll be perfectly safe. Ready?'

She nodded and tensed as he moved away slowly.

'Relax,' he called over his shoulder.

He drove the bike out around the streets to let her get the feel of being a pillion passenger until he felt her begin to relax, and then he slowly increased his speed. As they left the town and headed for the country, she felt exhilarated. Sam's body sheltered her from the wind and she leaned against his back. As they cornered, she leaned with him and the bike until she felt at one with him and his machine. They turned off the main road and she read the sign – Hillhead – and then she knew why she would need a swimsuit as they headed down the road leading to the beach.

Sam parked the bike and helped her off the back. Her legs felt stiff, and she staggered against him. He caught hold of her and laughed. 'You'll soon get used to it,' he said. 'Can you swim?'

'Yes, I love swimming.'

'Good, that'll help loosen those muscles.' He opened the panniers of the bike and took out a towel and packed sandwiches, plus a couple of bottles of lemonade. 'Come on,' he said and led her to a spot among the sand dunes.

It was a warm balmy day and they took off their coats and undressed beneath their towels, before heading for the water, running down the sand and both plunging into the waves.

Sam was a strong swimmer, she discovered, but he made sure she could keep up with him, never pushing her beyond her limits. They cavorted in the water, splashing each other before eventually returning to their place in the dunes. Sam rubbed her down with her towel, before insisting he cover her with sun oil.

'I can't have you getting burnt,' he insisted.

Not that Connie minded, feeling his strong hands on her back, arms and legs. Then he pulled her to him and kissed her soundly. 'I've been wanting to do that since you stepped out of your house,' he said. 'I've missed you, lovely Connie.'

She kissed him back. 'I've missed you too.'

'Come on, let's eat,' he said, 'I'm starving!'

They tucked into the sandwiches and some fruit he'd packed, then lay back enjoying the warmth of the sun as it dried them.

Sam told her of the car he'd been working on and about a forthcoming race, then he asked her what she'd been doing.

'Nothing exciting,' she lied. 'Just work.'

He gathered her into his arms. 'Well, I'm back now and I don't think I'm away again for some time.' He pulled her closer. 'I've got a week to make up for.'

Connie was pleased they'd found a quiet place not overlooked by others as his kisses became more fervent and his caresses more intimate. But there was a tenderness about him as he touched her, as if she was someone to be cherished and nurtured. There was a limit to his caresses, making sure he had her approval.

As for Connie, her body cried out for him, but she couldn't let him know in case it spoiled his illusion of her. She felt she would have disappointed him.

He caressed her cheek and stared deep into her eyes. 'Oh, Connie, if only you were a little older.'

'What on earth do you mean?' she asked.

'I so want to make love to you, but I have to respect your innocence.'

What was she to do? She longed for him with an ache that was unbearable, but he thought of her as untouched. She gazed back at him. 'Someone has to teach me how to be a woman,' she said softly.

He chuckled and said, 'This is true, sweetheart, and it would be my pleasure, but let's not rush things. We have plenty of time to get to know one another. Come on, let's go for a swim. I think it'll do us both good under the circumstances.'

Feeling totally frustrated, she followed him down to the water and plunged in. At least he'd called her sweetheart, and that was something.

On the way home, they stopped off at a restaurant in Lyndhurst for a meal, and whilst
they ate Sam told her a little more about
tourist car racing, of his dreams of becoming
a racing driver as a profession as well as own-
ing his own business, dealing strictly with
racing cars, and she realized just how deeply
he cared about this world of which she knew
nothing.

'But isn't it dangerous?' she asked with a
worried frown.

'Yes, I won't lie to you. It isn't the safest of
occupations, but I could be run over by a
car in Southampton's High Street,' he pro-
claimed. 'I'm good at what I do, Connie. I
get behind a wheel of a car and I'm focused
on the race ahead. It's not something you
can do lightly.' He paused. 'Do you think
you can understand how I feel about racing?
Because if you're going to be my girl, you
have to take me warts and all.' He took her
hand in his. 'Well?'

'Whatever you did, Sam, I would still want
to be with you.' She squeezed his hand.

He beamed at her. 'That's wonderful! But
I have to warn you, when there is a race
looming I have to spend a great deal of time
working on the car, which means if you
want to be with me you'll have to spend a
lot of hours hanging around the garage. It's

a lot to ask of a girl.'

'Not if she really likes you.'

'I'm so glad you said that. Come on, let's get the bill and we had better get you home. How about taking in a film tomorrow night? It helps me relax after a hard day, and at least I get to hold you in the dark.'

'That would be lovely,' she agreed.

Outside her house, Sam took her into his arms and kissed her. 'We are going to have some exciting times together, lovely Connie. I'll meet you outside the cinema at six thirty tomorrow.' He put his finger under her chin and tipped her face upwards. 'And if some other man comes on to you, tell him you are already spoken for. Right?'

'Right!' she said and kissed him.

She watched him drive away and went inside, smiling to herself.

'Have a good time?' asked her mother. Her father peered over his paper at her, waiting for her answer.

'Lovely!' she said. 'We went to Hillhead and had a picnic then swam. On the way home we stopped for a meal.'

George Morgan spoke. 'Someone was telling me in the pub about your boyfriend,' he said. 'Seems he's a good driver and a bit of a star on the racing track.'

Connie was delighted. 'Really?'

'Yes, seems he's got a future there. I hope

he doesn't drive fast when he takes you out, Connie?'

'No need to worry, Dad, he takes good care of me. He's a safe driver on the roads, I promise.'

Her father disappeared behind his paper.

Connie glanced across at her grandmother, waiting for her usual comment, but to her surprise the old woman remained silent.

Four

When Connie arrived at work the following day, she knew that John Baker would have returned from his holiday. She was still furious that her lover had made no reference to going away during their weekend in Bournemouth, and she was anxious that now he'd slept with her he'd ignore her, which would make her feel cheap and used. But she still maintained a modicum of pride and steeled herself as she saw him walking towards the counter, looking as dapper as ever, but with a tan, which only added to his attraction.

'Good morning, Connie, how are you today?'

She studied him intently. He was smiling warmly and seemed genuinely pleased to see her.

'Good morning, Mr Baker,' she said politely. 'Did you have a nice holiday with your family?'

He frowned at the distant tone in her voice. 'Thank you, I did. Susan loves playing on a beach, and as you know–' he paused – 'my one concern is to please my daughter.'

She met his gaze coldly. 'No doubt Mrs Baker enjoyed it too!'

He stiffened and, staring behind her at the shelves displaying various items, he said sharply, 'You need to replenish your stock, Connie, before the morning rush. You'd better come with me to the stockroom,' and he walked away.

She had no choice but to follow him.

She waited for him to unlock the door and followed him inside, where he promptly slammed the door shut behind them. Grabbing her by the arm he asked, 'What on earth was all that about?'

'I don't know what you mean,' she protested, her heart beating wildly. She'd never seen him so angry.

'Of course you do! What are you on your high horse about?'

All her inner torment poured forth. 'You take me away to Bournemouth, you make love to me, dump me at the station like an old rag and go off on holiday without even mentioning it to me! What am I supposed to think?'

He began to relax as he loosened his hold. 'I didn't mention it to you, darling, because it would have spoilt the wonderful time we were having, and I wanted it to be special, that's all, and as for leaving you at the station, if our relationship is to survive, we can't possibly be seen together. I'm well-known in the town, Connie. I didn't want to put you in a compromising position, because I care about you.'

'You do?' This took her by surprise, and now she was confused.

He took her into his arms. 'Of course I do, darling. You are something very precious in my life.'

'Really?' She couldn't help the note of sarcasm in her voice. He tilted her chin upwards and softly kissed her. 'How could you ever doubt it?'

Before she could answer, he put his hand in his pocket and withdrew a small jeweller's box. 'I bought this for you.'

She was shocked into silence as she looked at it.

'Don't you want to know what's inside?'

She took the box from him. Opening it she saw a gold chain with a locket shaped like a heart. She gazed up at him, speechless.

Chuckling softly, John took the chain from the box and said, 'Here, let me put it on for you.' He turned her round and fastened the clasp then softly kissed the back of her neck.

'Come on,' he said, 'let's get the stock or people will begin to wonder, and we don't want that, do we?'

'No,' said Connie, 'and thank you, it's beautiful.' What else could she say? She could hardly hand it back, that would have seemed so rude.

As they returned to the counter with the goods to be stacked she was in a state of flux... So he did think about her and ... and he wanted a relationship! So she did mean something to him after all! But did she want to carry on with this affair, now she had met Sam, who was so different and who didn't have a wife and child in the background? She couldn't think straight.

For the rest of the day, she kept fingering the heart, trying to make up her mind, until Betty commented, 'For God's sake Connie, will you leave that bloody thing around your neck alone? You'll wear it away, and where did you get it, anyway? I've never seen it before and I know all your bits of jewellery!'

'I treated myself to it from my wages,' she replied quickly and moved away.

Connie was unaware that the whole morning scenario had been carefully noted by Gillian Spencer, the manageress of the fashion department, situated on the opposite side of the same floor. Her eyes had narrowed as John had led the young assistant away. Now what was he up to, she wondered. But when she saw them return, carrying various items, she was in no doubt. The stock room had been a place where she and Baker had sneaked into on occasion when she had been his 'flavour of the month'.

Their affair had been a torrid one, and as she had her own flat, meeting with him had been easy; working late had been a simple excuse for him to give to his wife. Then when Kay had given birth to his daughter, Gillian realized that any hopes of a future with this man were never going to materialize. When he started to cool off and had put an end to their relationship, she put the whole thing behind her and moved on, and when, sometime later, he'd approached her again, she'd had the willpower to refuse his advances.

'But we were so good together,' he'd said.

For a moment she'd been tempted, remembering how he'd made her feel when he held her in his arms and made love to her. Oh, he was so accomplished between the sheets. He made her lose all of her inhibitions, and she had thrived on his attention. But, looking at him, she also remembered how cold he was when he'd told her it was over.

'Yes we were good together, but that was then,' she told him. 'Now I'm not interested. You were just an experience!'

How good it had made her feel to see the anger in his eyes just before she walked away from him, feeling triumphant at his discomfort. Nevertheless, knowing all this didn't stop that small part of her wanting him still. Now he was working his charm on the young girl working in the haberdashery department. A mere child! Should she have a quiet word with her? Warn her that John was a known philanderer? She tried to put herself in the girl's place. If someone had done that to her at the time, she knew it wouldn't have made any difference. This man had too much charisma, and this girl wasn't as worldly at her young age, but she knew eventually John would tire of the girl and move on. He always did. She turned away as a customer approached her.

Towards the end of the day, John stopped by Connie's counter and quietly said, 'Meet me in the park by the big rockery. I've missed you so much, I need to see you,' and he walked away. She didn't have a chance to answer so she felt obliged to do as he asked. She thought if she did see him, it would help her decide what to do in the future. She didn't want to risk losing her new boyfriend, but John only had to touch her and she felt helpless. He was the first man she'd slept with, and somehow that felt almost as if she was bound to him in some way.

After leaving work, she walked slowly to the park, her mind in turmoil. Common sense told her to stop this liaison, it could only end in tears, someone would end up getting hurt, so was it worth the risk? Yet she still remembered how John made her feel when, in Bournemouth, he took her to bed and introduced her to sex. She'd loved to feel his hands, his mouth on her body. It had been an amazing experience, and if she was honest, she wanted it again and again. The very fact that it was illicit only added to the excitement of it all. How wicked was that, she thought. But at the same time it was rather delicious! She waited.

John arrived shortly after and, taking her by the hand, led her to a bench behind the rockery which hid them from sight of any passers-by. He took her into his arms and kissed her hungrily.

'God!' he muttered. 'You feel so good.' And he kissed her again.

Connie lost herself to all the physical sensations that flooded through her. Oh, it felt so good to be in his arms again, and she wished they were in a bedroom somewhere where they could take this further. She closed her eyes as he caressed her and kissed her again and again. All doubts left her. She couldn't let him go, she couldn't!

In the Chapel area of the town, Sam was facing his own problems. Someone had tried to break into the garage overnight. The locks had been tampered with, and there were marks on the door where, fortunately, it had withstood whatever tool had been used to try and force it open. He and his men had no doubt who was at the root of all this. The thing now was – what to do about it?

'We can go round there mob-handed and break their bloody legs,' raged Harry.

'Cool down, for goodness' sake, Sam urged. 'We have no proof it was Jake and his boys, and anyway that wouldn't solve anything and would only get us into trouble with the law. We have to think of something constructive.'

'Well, I suggest we move the car to a different venue – under cover, of course. Let them believe it's here. At least that will give us a place of safety, because it's obvious this isn't any more,' Tom said.

'Got anywhere in mind?' Sam asked.

'As a matter of fact I have. A mate of mine has an empty garage in Shirley. We could hire that from him.'

'Would he keep his mouth shut? Otherwise there would be no point at all in moving.'

Tom grinned broadly. 'You could trust him with your life, Sam. You are his hero. He follows every race you've ever entered. He'd feel privileged to help you.'

Raising his eyebrows in surprise, Sam said, 'Really? Have I ever met him?'

Shaking his head, Tom said, 'No. He's been too shy to approach you, but I know he'd be only too pleased to help out. He's not a bad mechanic either. He's into motor-bikes himself.'

'Then have a word with him today. I think we'd better keep a watch on this place tonight. I don't want to leave the car unprotected, and I'll have a word with the local bobby to keep his eyes open when he does his rounds.'

Young Jimmy Murphy was delighted when he was asked to come to Sam's aid. So, in the dead of night, the car was moved to its new home. The streets were empty as the Riley Pathfinder was towed away, and Jimmy was waiting, overcome with excitement, at his garage. He'd cleared and cleaned the interior, all ready for the arrival of Sam and his vehicle.

Sam shook his hand and thanked him profusely for helping them out.

The young man was so overcome with having his hero there, he stumbled over his words. 'That's fine, just fine.' He pranced on the spot, unable to keep still. 'If you want an extra pair of hands, Mr Knight, I'll be happy to help you out.'

'Please call me Sam, and thanks, Jimmy, we can always use a good mechanic.'

Jimmy was in seventh heaven and, scratching his head, he muttered, 'Bloody Hell!'

They locked up the garage after a full inspection. It was sturdily built and with new locks was deemed safe. They all left to go home and sleep.

As Sam climbed into bed, he realized that he had to decide whether to tell Connie what had transpired and let her into the secret. He'd wait a while, he thought, and see how things went. He didn't want her involved at the moment, knowing how devious Jake Barton could be. No, it was probably safer to keep her out of the loop for the time being.

To Connie's surprise, Sam called into Tyrell and Greens the following day and found her department.

'Hello,' he said, smiling at the shocked expression on her face when she saw him.

'Whatever are you doing here?' she asked.

'I had some business to attend to so I thought I'd give you a surprise. Are you free this evening? Only, I thought we could go and have a meal somewhere.'

She beamed at him with pleasure. 'I'd love to.'

'Good, I'll wait for you at the staff entrance. What time do you finish?'

'About a quarter past six.'

He gazed around the shop floor at all the displays and then back at her, taking in her neat white blouse and black skirt. 'It's strange seeing you in your workplace, it's as if I'm looking at a different girl,' he teased.

'Which one do you prefer?' she asked with eyes twinkling. 'I'll have to compare the two and let you know.' He grinned at her. 'I'll see you later.'

Betty, who had been watching the

encounter, sidled up to her friend. 'Don't tell me. That was Sam, yes?'

Connie nodded. 'He's taking me out for a meal after work.'

'Very nice too! It's time you found someone decent.'

As she went about her work, Connie knew that her friend spoke the truth, but she was torn between her conscience and lust. She was playing a dangerous game, she was aware of that. She risked both John's wife and Sam discovering her guilty secret. Strangely, the latter bothered her more than the former. In her heart she realized she wasn't the first conquest of the floor manager – she'd heard the rumours about his roving eye when she first joined the staff, and if they were true, Mrs Baker would be an idiot not to suspect – but once she'd foolishly accepted his first invitation and been held in his arms, she shut her mind to anything else. But Sam ... Sam was a decent, honest man, and she felt he'd be appalled if he were to find out about her sexual encounters. He'd kissed her passionately but he'd never caressed her too intimately, which showed his respect for her as a young woman. Not that she thought for one moment he was without experience. The way he kissed her was certainly not the kiss of a novice.

Just before the store closed, John Baker

wandered over to Connie and asked, 'Are you doing anything this evening?'

Betty, who was standing nearby, intervened: 'She's going out with her boyfriend!' She walked away grinning broadly.

John's face was like thunder. 'Boyfriend! What boyfriend?'

Connie suddenly felt empowered. For so long she'd been at this man's beck and call, meeting him whenever he demanded, going willingly to him. Enjoying the excitement of this extramarital relationship. It had made her feel daring and mature. However now someone else wanted to be with her, a man without baggage, a man who treated her tenderly. For once, she had the upper hand.

'My boyfriend. He's a racing driver, and he cares about me!'

'I care about you,' he said quietly.

'So you say, but after all, John, you can't expect me to just sit about and wait for your call. You go home to your wife, so why can't I have a boyfriend?'

His face flushed with anger. 'Leave my wife out of it.' He was called away at that moment, which put an end to their conversation.

Connie walked over to her friend. 'Thanks a bunch!'

'I'm just being a pal, that's all. Now I've seen Sam I hate to see you mixed up with that lecherous bugger even more. When he's finished with you, he'll drop you without a second thought. Had you stayed with him, you'd be devastated. Get out now! Move on with Sam, he's a lovely bloke. Don't be silly or you'll lose both of them!'

When John Baker walked into his house that evening, Kay, his wife, took one look at his expression and remained silent. If he'd had a bad day at the shop he would tell her over dinner; if he said nothing, then things were not going well with his new affair! She had no illusions about her husband. When first they met she knew he was a flirt, but she'd fallen deeply in love with him and when he'd proposed she didn't hesitate to accept.

For the first few years, they'd been ideally happy, and when Susan had been born, their happiness was complete. But a new baby was tiring, and Kay had been too weary to respond to his advances in bed for a while. During that time, she knew he'd taken a lover. However, she was certain that his real love for her hadn't diminished, and as the affairs escalated, she had to make a decision. Should she shut her eyes to it all? After all, he was always attentive, indeed more so during such liaisons, and his love for his daughter was without question. If she put her suspicions into words, what would happen to their marriage? His adultery never lasted for long, so had no real meaning to him, and he always made sure the bills were paid and that she had a personal allowance. She had decided that, with a child, she couldn't jeopardize this security and so shut her mind to his philandering. But as the years passed it was becoming more difficult to accept. Who was it this time, she wondered.

John took Susan up to bed and read her a story, as was his habit whilst Kay prepared the meal. Kissing Susan goodnight, he went downstairs, poured himself a drink and sat at the table as his wife served the meal.

'Had a busy day?' she asked.

'No more than usual, how about you?'

So it was a woman, she thought as she told him about her day. As she did so, she studied the man whom she'd married seven years ago. He was good looking, well dressed and he'd always had an air of sophistication about him, even as a young man. Yes, she could see how attractive he would be to other women, but that was no excuse for his infidelity. How would he feel, she wondered, if *she* took a lover? The very thought amused her. All her life she'd lived by the rules even as a child. She believed in her marriage vows ... what a pity her husband didn't feel the same, and she wondered for a moment what it would feel like to be held in another man's arms.

'What are you smiling at?' John asked.

The sudden interruption to her train of thought brought her back to reality. She hadn't realized she'd smiled at the thoughts of her own adultery and she started to chuckle. 'Oh, it was just something Susan said today that amused me.' And the moment passed.

Five

There was to be a major race at Silverstone a month hence and Sam and his mates were working hard on his Riley Pathfinder in their new premises, with the added help of Jimmy Murphy, who turned out to be a good mechanic. The race was over sixteen laps with a good pot for the winner at the end. Sam was working on the engine, fine-tuning it to produce the maximum speed that he'd require to beat off the competition. There was also a lot of work to do on the interior to make it safe and secure should there be a crash. The three men worked in silence each concentrating on the job in hand. Eventually, stiff and sore from so much bending, they took a break. All stretched their cramped limbs, before sitting down with a cigarette and a cup of tea.

'Heard anything of Jake Barton?' Sam asked.

Tom shook his head. 'No, he's keeping a low profile these days. His garage is always under lock and key, door shut. I know because I wander past from time to time. We don't even know what type of vehicle he'll be driving.'

With a grin Sam said, 'Well, it'll have to be

something special to beat this baby,' and he patted the door of his car.

Nodding his agreement, Tom remarked, 'He'll have a bloody fit when he sees the speed you can reach now we've worked on the engine. He won't like it.'

'He'll have a good view of my tail lights all through the sixteen laps. By the end he'll be as sick as a pig!'

'I don't trust that bugger,' muttered Harry. 'If he can't win by fair means, he'll look for another way. We need to watch our backs.'

Sam discounted their concerns. 'We've managed so far. He hasn't realized we've moved the workshop so he can't tamper with the car. His only chance is to take me out on the track and I'm all ready for that; after all, he's not very subtle about his driving, is he?'

'True,' agreed Harry, 'but even that bastard can get lucky.'

Getting to his feet Sam urged his mates to return to their work. 'Barton can take his chances with all the others,' he said. 'I'm the one who's going to stand on the winner's podium if I've anything to do with it!'

That evening he waited for Connie, and they walked along the waterfront on to the pier and sat on one of the benches, drinking coffee. He told her about the forthcoming race and how important it was.

'If I can win this one, it'll be a step up in

my career,' he told her. 'The racing authorities will have no choice but to recognize me as a major driver.'

'My dad was telling me you already have made a name for yourself on the racetrack,' she said proudly.

'Did he?' He looked pleased. 'Well, without sounding bigheaded, he's right, but I want to be among the big boys, not a big fish in a small pond. This takes time and success. You're only as good as your last race, I'm afraid.'

Connie frowned. 'Don't you feel scared when you're tearing around a track with other cars trying to take you out?'

Shaking his head he said, 'No. Waiting on the starting line for the flag to go down, adrenalin is pumping through your veins and all you want is to go, then it's total concentration until the finish. Then if you win, it's euphoria you feel, not fear. If racing scares you, it's the wrong thing to be doing.'

She didn't look convinced.

He tried to explain. 'I feel nervous, of course, so does every other driver, but that's a different thing, Connie. I know my car is safe because I and my boys have made it so – so the main danger is from the other cars in the race, or rather the drivers of the other cars.'

'Why, because they aren't any good?'

He chuckled. 'Oh no! They all know what

they're doing, it's the way that they do it. I'm afraid there are some who are villains at the wheel who have no scruples at all as to how they win a race, but you needn't worry about them. I know who they are and am always aware of them around me.'

She gazed at him with concern in her eyes. 'I would hate anything bad to happen to you, Sam.'

He gently stroked her face. 'What a lovely thing to say, but don't you worry, sweetheart. I've been in this game too long to take stupid chances. There are always tricks of the trade, whatever it is – and I know them all. Come on, I'll take you home.'

Outside her house Sam took Connie into his arms and kissed her. 'You are very sweet,' he said 'and I love the fact you are my girl. I like knowing I'll be seeing you regularly, holding you, kissing you ... wanting you.'

'Do you want me, Sam?' she asked, snuggling into him, her hands beneath his jacket, stroking his back.

'Oh yes, Connie, I do. But you're very precious to me and I'd be a heel if I took advantage of you.'

'Even if I agreed?'

Tipping her chin upwards, he looked at her with an intensity that she found thrilling. He was fighting his need for her, and she wished so very much that he wouldn't because she wanted him to make love to her.

'I want you too Sam,' she said, and she kissed him passionately.

No man could resist her invitation, and he returned her kisses with a fervour, exploring her mouth, his hand caressing her breast until he pulled away.

'You're not playing fair!' he said, holding her firmly away from him.

'But don't you see, if I want the same thing, you won't be taking advantage of me. I want you to love me.'

He studied her face, wondering if she meant what she said and saw the longing in her expression. 'Very well, sweetheart. When we race next month, you come with us. We'll stay overnight in a hotel after the race ... if that's what you *really* want.'

She wound her arms around his neck. 'More than anything.'

Connie didn't tell Betty of her conversation with Sam and their plans. She wanted to keep that a secret between her and her boy-friend. For her it was something special with no complications. Sam didn't have a wife in the background, and he considered her youth, whereas John Baker hadn't. He was the one who'd taken advantage of her, had carefully taken her down his path until in Bournemouth he'd achieved his aim. It was true she'd not fought off his advances but he certainly was no gentleman to have encouraged her. Now perhaps she could find the courage to let him go.

She needn't have worried about Betty. Her friend was full of the trial of Ruth Ellis, who had been found guilty of murdering her boyfriend and had been sentenced to hang.

'You need to be careful, Connie! What if Mrs Baker finds out about you and her husband?'

Connie glared at her. 'Don't be ridiculous!'

'I'm only warning you,' her friend insisted.

Kay Baker was in the town shopping and, feeling weary, decided to go into Tyrell and Greens for a coffee, then after she'd see if she could see her husband and find out what he wanted for his dinner as she had yet to buy the food for that evening.

She left the restaurant and wandered around the store, looking at the goods on the ground floor, then made her way up the stairs to look for John. She saw him in the distance and started in his direction. He was walking towards the haberdashery, a set expression on his face. She immediately thought that a member of the staff had displeased him and watched to see what would happen.

She saw him waylay a young woman behind the counter. There seemed to be a heated conversation going on between them in low voices. Oh dear, she thought, she's in

77

trouble. He grabbed the girl by the wrist, but she snatched her hand away, said something to him, then walked off. It all suddenly fell into place, and Kay was shaken. This was his new amour! For God's sake the girl was years younger than he was! What did he think he was playing at?

Connie was fuming! Her lover had demanded she wait for him after work, and she'd refused. She said she was meeting her boyfriend, and he'd been furious. She rubbed her wrist where he'd held her. He had no right to tell her what to do. Cancel her appointment with Sam! Not likely. She'd told John to get lost, and she thought he was going to have a fit. Well, serve him right. She looked up as a customer stood before her.

'Can I help you, madam?'

Kay Baker looked at the girl and said, 'I need two yards of two-inch elastic, please.'

'Certainly,' Connie said and went to find some.

Kay watched her. Yes she was pretty, had a good figure, nice hair ... and she hated her! This girl was coming between her and her marriage. She'd never seen any of her husband's lovers before and was astonished at the strength of her feelings. She wanted to slap her, tell her she had no right to mess up her life. As Connie returned with the elastic,

78

she took a deep breath to try and calm down.

'Is there anything else, madam?'

Kay's eyes flashed with anger. 'Yes. Leave my husband alone!'

Connie was startled. 'Pardon?'

'I am the wife of John Baker. Leave my husband alone ... is that clear enough?'

Connie paled and her hands shook. 'Yes, madam – er, Mrs Baker.'

'Good.' Kay walked quickly away, shaking with anger, and astounded at her own actions. *Oh my God! What have I done?* she asked herself. Nevertheless, she didn't regret it one bit. She'd had enough. She decided no longer would she turn a blind eye to her husband's shenanigans.

Connie watched her go, still trembling. Bloody hell! That was such a shock. To actually come face to face with a wronged wife – *and* for her to know that she was seeing her husband. Betty's warning rang in her ears. Connie suddenly felt sick and rushed away to the ladies room and threw up!

That evening, Connie left the store, still suffering from shock, and when she saw Sam standing waiting for her she flew into his arms and clung on tightly.

He held on to her, feeling her shaking in his arms. 'Connie! Whatever is the matter?'

How could she tell him? She couldn't. 'I've just had a bad day,' she hastily lied. 'My boss bawled me out and I was upset. That's all.'

'It must have been pretty bad, sweetheart. Look at the state of you. What on earth had you done?'

'I'd just priced some goods up incorrectly and sold a few under the price.' She was amazed how quickly the lies flew from her mouth. 'But I'm all right now you're here.'

'No one has the right to cause this kind of reaction. I'll have a word with him!'

How hilarious would that be, she thought. Then looking at Sam she smiled and kissed his cheek. 'My Mr Knight in shining armour! Where's your white horse then?'

Chuckling he said, 'Over there,' pointing to his motorbike. 'Come on, let's eat and then you can tell me all about it.'

'No, just let's eat and you can tell me about *your* day.'

She climbed on to the back of Sam's bike and put on the helmet he handed to her, placed her arms around his waist and leaned against him. How comforting it was, she thought. With Sam she felt safe.

John Baker watched them drive away. So that was the boyfriend. He was consumed with jealousy. He'd not yet had his fill of young Connie. He certainly wasn't ready to dispense with her yet, not after spending money on a hotel so he could claim her virginity. That had been something new. Most of his

80

previous affairs had been with experienced women, and he'd enjoyed the fact that he was the one to teach such a willing girl all about the pleasures of the flesh.

As he made his way home he pictured the man with Connie. He looked vaguely familiar, and he wracked his brain to try and remember why this should be ... then he remembered she'd said he was a racing driver. That was it! There had been an article in the local paper about him and about his success on the racetrack. So ... this was no ordinary chap. It only served to add to his displeasure. He walked on in a thoroughly bad frame of mind, which was not dispelled when he walked through the door of his house and found his wife waiting for him.

Six

Kay Baker was cooking in her kitchen after bathing Susan and getting her ready for her nightly story with her father. She was feeling very tense. She'd made up her mind to confront her husband after dinner and she had no way of knowing how the evening would end. But she'd had enough. Tonight was make or break time.

John let himself into the house, hung up his coat, gave his wife a perfunctory kiss, picked up his daughter, hugged her and said, 'Ready for bed and your story?'

The child squealed with delight. 'The three bears, Daddy, please.'

In the kitchen, Kay poured herself a sherry to give her some Dutch courage and laid the table. Hearing footsteps coming down the stairs, she took a large gulp of alcohol, carried the serving dishes into the dining room and sat down.

John sat at the table and helped himself to some vegetables then poured gravy over the lamb chops on his plate, followed by mint sauce. He glanced up as he held out the sauce to Kay. He was surprised to see her just sitting watching him.

'Something wrong?' he snapped.

'I see you're in a bad mood but there's no need to use that tone of voice to me just because your girlfriend's upset you!'

He looked at her in astonishment. Not once in all the years they'd been married, despite his numerous affairs, had his wife ever mentioned another woman to him.

'What on earth are you talking about?'

'The young girl on the haberdashery. I saw you with her today.'

'You what?'

'I was in town shopping. I popped into the store for a coffee and came looking for you, just in time to see the argument between you both.'

'Oh that!' he bluffed. 'I had to admonish her about her rudeness to a customer who'd complained.'

'You do surprise me,' she said quietly. 'I found her very polite.'

'You spoke to her?'

'Yes, she served me.'

He tried to laugh her accusations away. 'For goodness' sake, Kay, you're jumping to ridiculous conclusions.'

She looked scornfully at him. 'She didn't find it ridiculous when I told her to leave my husband alone. I thought she was going to faint. That and her look of guilt was enough to know I *wasn't* mistaken. For Christ's sake John, she's a *child!*'

He didn't know what to say. He'd convinced himself his wife was unaware of his adultery; indeed, he had always been so careful to make sure she'd had no reason to think that their marriage was other than secure. He looked at her and was at a loss for words.

Kay, however, wasn't. Years of frustration at shutting her eyes to his infidelity poured forth. 'You must think I'm a complete fool! I've always known you've had other women! You come home and climb into our bed reeking of a strange perfume and think I won't notice. The excuses of working late, so often when you had someone, but regular hours when you were *between* women!' She glared at him. 'I have known about every single one, but today was the first time I'd ever seen the woman concerned – and I've had enough!'

'What do you mean, you've had enough?' Now he was worried.

'You want someone else, then fine! Pack your bags and go to them. Let them take care of you, cook for you, do your dirty washing. Look after you until you get bored and move on to the next one. Me ... I won't put up with you and your women any longer! In fact, do it now, I can't bear to even look at you!' She rose from the table and walked into the kitchen.

He was up like a shot and followed her. 'Now, Kay, you're being silly.'

She turned on him with fury. 'You're *not*

going to deny it all, I hope? Please don't insult my intelligence.'

He put out his hand towards her. She snatched her arm away.

'Don't you dare touch me! Go and find your little girl and see if she'll take you in. I'll make an appointment to see my solicitor in the morning.'

He was reeling from the acceleration of the situation. This was getting completely out of hand and he was now desperate.

'Look, darling, I'm really sorry. I know I've done wrong and you didn't deserve the way I've treated you, but I don't want to leave you and Susan. I love you both, surely you know that?'

She leaned against the kitchen sink and saw the desperation in his eyes. 'But not enough to keep your marriage vows, John. Well, you've made your own choice and now I've made mine. You, of course, will have visitation rights to see Susan. I don't want her life ruined by all this. And you will make sure we have enough to live on and you will cover the mortgage as usual.'

He was flabbergasted. 'You've got it all worked out, haven't you!' Now he was angry.

But Kay was in control. 'Please don't use that outraged tone with me, John. I've put up with the knowledge of your extramarital relationships for too many years. If anyone should be outraged it's me! Now, please, pack an overnight bag. I'll have the rest of your stuff packed tomorrow. You can come and pick it up in your lunch hour when Susan's at nursery school.'

She met his gaze uncompromisingly, and he had no choice but to do her bidding. And half an hour later, Kay watched the tail lights of his car disappear down the road and burst into tears.

In a daze, John Baker drove to the Star Hotel and booked a room. He sat on the edge of the bed wondering what on earth had happened to Kay, who was always gentle and kind and who had changed into a whirling dervish! The very fact she'd discovered that he was seeing Connie and had exchanged words with her was even more shocking.

He lit a cigarette and puffed slowly and deeply. His marriage was in ruins! She'd ordered him out of the house! Letting out a sigh, he put his hand to his head, unable to believe what had happened. What was he going to do?

He left the room and went to the bar, ordering a double scotch and soda. Then he sat quietly trying to plan his next move. He *had* to get Kay to change her mind. Despite his philanderings, he loved his home, family life. Adored his daughter, and Kay was the perfect wife. The other... It didn't mean anything. Surely, she must know that?

In the kitchen of the marital home, Kay wiped her tears and drank the remains of the sherry. Walking upstairs, she peered into Susan's room and saw her child was fast asleep, then she went into her bedroom, took a large suitcase from under the bed and started to pack her husband's clothes.

Despite her anger, she was worried. She'd made her stand and now she'd have to live with the consequences. What if John decided to be difficult over the financial arrangement? How would she live? No, he wouldn't do that, she thought. Even if he didn't care about her he'd want to look after Susan's welfare. Her solicitor would advise her, she decided.

She dreaded tomorrow when John'd return for the rest of his belongings. What sort of a mood would he be in? No matter what, she determined, she wouldn't change her mind. Why should she? She'd put up with him for far too long. Now *she* would have a life!

That morning, Connie entered the staff entrance of the store and removed her coat. She was terrified of seeing her lover. Had his wife told him of their conversation? If so, what would he say? If not, and he wanted to meet her, what could she say? She certainly didn't want to face Mrs Baker again and be accused of consorting with her husband.

Her hands were trembling at the thought, and she dropped a load of goods.

'What on earth's the matter with you this morning?' demanded Betty. 'You're all of a dither!'

'I didn't sleep well, that's all,' she answered and carried on. Then, across the floor, she saw John striding quickly across towards her counter. He sent Betty to the stockroom on an errand, then glared at Connie.

'What on earth did you say to my wife yesterday?' He looked at her coldly.

'I didn't say anything! I thought she was a customer. She asked for some elastic and then when I asked if there was anything else, she told me to keep away from her husband!'

'And what did you say?'

'I didn't say anything!' Now Connie was getting angry. It was bad enough to be accused by the wife, but now John was behaving as if it were all her fault. 'What did you expect me to say? Tell her about our weekend in Bournemouth, registered as your wife!'

He paled visibly at her outburst. 'Keep your voice down,' he hissed.

'She told you about our meeting then?'

His lips narrowed. 'Oh yes, she certainly did. She ordered me out of the house.'

Connie studied the angry man before her and suddenly saw him in a different light. He was no longer the charmer who had led her astray. He was a man with an appetite who'd

88

been found out. An unattractive creature –
and she knew at once she was free of him at
last.

'Is there anything else?' She looked at him
as if he were a stranger who had just dropped
by.

'Is that all you can say? My marriage is in
ruins!'

'That's your problem, John. Not mine,' she
said, and she turned away to serve a customer.

At lunchtime, Baker drove home and parked
in front of the door. Putting his key in the
lock, he struggled with it. What the hell was
wrong? The door opened, and Kay looked at
him.

'You're wasting your time. I've had the
locks changed!' She turned and walked into
the kitchen.

He followed. 'You what?' He didn't wait
for an answer. 'Was that really necessary?'

'I thought so.' She pointed into the corner.
'There are a couple of suitcases with your
clothes.' She handed him a carrier bag. 'And
here's your dirty washing!'

He looked at her in horror. 'What am I
supposed to do with this?'

She chuckled. 'I have no idea, but I suggest you don't wear it as it is.'

'This is not a laughing matter, Kay! You
are putting our marriage in danger.'

She was incredulous. *'I* am putting our marriage in danger? How can you stand there and say that? *You!* You have done this. You and your bloody women, so don't try and lay the blame at *my* door!'

His mind was racing nineteen to the dozen trying to think of a way to change the situation. 'You're right, and I've been a fool. But, Kay, darling, I don't want to lose you. I still love you, surely you know that?'

She looked scornfully at him. 'Frankly, I don't give a damn, as Rhett Butler once said. You see, John ... I no longer love you. In fact, I've not loved you for quite a while.'

This shocked him to his core. 'What? I don't believe you.'

'Please yourself. Years ago when I first found out about your womanizing, I made a decision to stay with you, but after every affair, my love died a little bit more. Now all I feel is anger. Not at you, strangely – but at myself for staying in this sham of a marriage for so long.' She glared at him, defiance burning in her eyes. 'I am going to divorce you on the grounds of adultery!'

He couldn't believe what he was hearing. 'You can't do that!'

'Indeed I can and I will, and what's more if you contest it I'll name your shop girl. I asked someone who she was so I know her name. Think of the scandal!'

The consequence of her remark horrified

him. 'I could lose my job!'

She shrugged. 'Not if you don't contest the case.'

His eyes narrowed. 'You seem pretty sure about all this.'

'I had a long conversation with my solicitor this morning. I'm not quite the fool you think I am. Seven years of marriage and you still think I'm only capable of being a wife and mother. Well, John my dear, I'm much more than that!'

He studied the stranger before him. He didn't know this woman at all. 'Is there someone else?' he asked suddenly. 'Have you met another man?'

Kay started to laugh. 'Really! I'm not like you. No, there is no one else involved, but I hope to meet someone in the future. Someone who is honest, who will think enough of me to be faithful, to appreciate me for the woman I really am. Not just an appendage.'

'You have never just been that to me, Kay.'

'Not to begin with I grant you, but certainly in the latter years. I looked after your every need, like a housekeeper. I pleasured your bed whenever you turned to me, which I hated, knowing you'd been with another woman, but I had Susan to think about.'

He had only one more weapon to use to try and save his marriage and that was his daughter. 'Well, think of her now, I beg you. If we part she'll be devastated. Who will be here to read her stories at night?'

'I will! You can see her regularly, we'll make an arrangement – and at her age she'll soon accept the change once I've talked to her.'

A frown furrowed his brow. 'What on earth will you say to her? I don't want her upset.'

Kay glared at him. 'You never gave her a thought when you climbed into bed with another woman, did you?'

What could he say?

Kay walked to the door. 'We have nothing more to say to each other, John. You'll hear from my solicitor. Now I'd like you to leave.'

John Baker picked up the two suitcases and walked to the front door, where he hesitated and turned to his wife to speak.

She opened the door. 'Goodbye John.'

He walked out of the house, put the cases in the car and drove away.

Seven

During the weeks that followed, Connie only saw John briefly as he went about his work. He neglected to visit the haberdashery department, but instead sent one of his under-managers over whenever necessary. Which worked well for both of them.

Betty was delighted when Connie told her she'd stopped seeing the floor manager, although she didn't tell her why. Betty didn't ask but was just grateful that her friend had seen sense at last. Had she known that Connie was planning to spend the night with Sam after the Silverstone race, she might have thought differently.

Sam and his mates were working on the new car most of the time, and Connie, who now knew about the move, spent a lot of her weekends at the other garage and had become part of the team, making tea and trying to be useful. Occasionally, she and Sam managed a trip to the cinema, or to go out for a drink after work. Their relationship grew, and she was known as Sam's girl by all his friends.

One Sunday they took the car out and road-tested it on a disused airfield, moving the vehicle on the back of a truck especially built for the job. The field was deserted and the wind blew across the neglected runway, which had weeds growing through the tarmac. The atmosphere was tense as Sam climbed into the driving seat and strapped himself in. Connie stood with Tom and Harry as they prepared to time the run.

Connie held her breath as Sam moved the car into position, revved the engine, signalled that he was ready ... then took off.

It moved like a streak of lightning, and the excitement of the two men beside her was palpable. When eventually Sam had finished his run, Tom pressed the button on the stopwatch he was holding and read it.

'Bloody hell!' he exclaimed. 'That's fucking amazing! Oops, sorry Connie!'

She just laughed because although she wasn't knowledgeable even she could see that this was a fast time.

Sam drove over towards them. Tom said nothing; he just showed Sam the watch. The two men grinned broadly at each other.

'We've bloody done it!' Tom yelled and picked Connie up and swung her round. Then, putting her down, he clasped Harry in his arms and the two men danced around in glee.

Climbing out of the car, Sam kissed Connie and shook hands with his friends. 'Gentlemen, I think we have a winner!'

'Silverstone is in the bag!' said Harry enthusiastically.

But Sam tried to calm him down. 'Nothing is ever in the bag, you know that. If for one moment we become overconfident, we could lose the race.'

But Tom and Harry were too excited to listen. 'I'd love to see Jake Barton's face when he realizes what speed we have achieved with this engine,' Tom said with a wide grin.

'We have to find out what vehicle he's entering before we can celebrate,' Sam warned. 'He, too, may have achieved as much.'

Harry gave a derisory laugh. 'Barton? He hasn't got the brains!'

Sam agreed. 'He hasn't, but don't forget he has two good mechanics working with him and they are no slouches.'

Connie listened to the exchange of words between the men. It was very evident that something special was happening, but she felt her stomach tighten at the mention of the other driver. He obviously was bad news, and it worried her. She now knew just how dangerous the race game was, without the threat of any added danger from unscrupulous drivers.

She watched as the car was once again loaded on to the truck and Tom and Harry got into the driver's cab, then she climbed on the back of Sam's motorbike. They all returned to the garage, where the Riley was unloaded and safely locked away. Then the four of them found a cafe in Shirley to eat.

They discussed the run in low tones so that no one could overhear their conversation. Turning to Connie, Sam said, 'You mustn't breathe a word of what you saw today, sweetheart, we don't want to let the cat out of the bag before the race. You do under-stand how important this is, don't you?'

'Of course,' she assured him.

'We won't even tell Jimmy. Not that I don't trust him, but he's young and in his enthu-siasm he might let something slip without meaning to. We'll just say there is more work needed to be done before we're satisfied.'

'Today was so thrilling, I can't wait for Silverstone,' she said.

He took her hand in his. 'Neither can I.'

She knew by his expression he wasn't referring to the race, and she felt even more excited as she smiled at him.

Jake Barton too was looking forward to Silverstone. He and his men had been work-ing on a Jaguar he'd bought for the race, and he felt at last he had a vehicle that would beat the living daylights out of Sam Knight. That was even more important to him than winning the race itself, such was his obses-sion with the other driver. This was a great concern to his mechanics, who were sitting together in a pub, discussing the forthcoming race over a pint of beer.

Charlie was the first to put his thoughts into words. 'For the first time ever we have a chance in this race at Silverstone, but that bloody lunatic could ruin it if he doesn't keep focused on the race itself. All he talks about is beating Knight, and that worries me!'

'My thoughts exactly!' agreed Bert. 'We've slogged our bloody guts out tuning that engine and working on the body to make it safe – but to what end?'

Sipping his beer Charlie was deep in thought. Putting down the glass he looked at his friend and said, 'If he screws up the race, I'm off! Unless he can show me he's a professional when it's the big time, I'm moving on.' He rubbed his chin. 'I haven't forgotten how he decked me ... for nothing!'

'Me too!' Bert agreed. 'There are others who will appreciate what we have to offer; we won't lose out if we put the word about.' He lit a cigarette. 'This race is his last chance.'

Unaware of the hostility felt by his two men, Jake was in his garage sitting in the driving seat of his Jaguar, slowly revving the engine, listening to it purr. Stroking the dashboard lovingly.

'You little beauty,' he murmured. 'With you I'm going to show that bastard, Knight, just how good a driver I am. It's time he was taken down a peg or two.' He started laughing until the tears ran down his cheeks.

Prior to the race the *Southampton Evening Echo* ran an article about the two local men who were entering. There was a picture of Sam and another of Jake Barton. The list of Sam's successes far outweighed his opposition, which only enraged Jake more as he read it and fuelled the overwhelming hatred he felt for his rival.

Connie was delighted, of course, as she and her father read it together in the sitting room, discussing the young man, her father filled with admiration for his achievements. He passed the paper over to Madge to look at. She glanced at it briefly and just sniffed.

George looked at his daughter and winked. 'Take no notice,' he whispered.

John Baker, now living in a rented flat, also read the paper that evening as he ate his spaghetti on toast. He studied the features of the good-looking young man in the picture and was consumed with jealousy. Not only was he missing the comforts of home, but he was also missing the sexual excitement of his affair with Connie. Now this Lothario would be getting what he thought of as his.

His wife, Kay, had been to her solicitor and filed for divorce. He *was* now allowed to see his daughter on alternative weekends, which was heartbreaking for him, although she seemed to have accepted that he was now living elsewhere, and Kay – Kay was cold and businesslike when he called. In the hopes that he could stop the divorce going through and return to the marital home, he'd not caused any difficulty over finances; besides, he didn't want his little girl to have to do without. He had taken Kay flowers on one occasion, but she'd refused them.

'That isn't necessary,' she'd said. 'The only thing I want from you is to meet my financial needs – nothing more.'

The weekend of the race, Kay was taking Susan away so he thought he'd go to Silverstone and watch, see what made this young chap so interesting. After all, he'd nothing else to do and these days his free time hung heavily, especially the weekend when he didn't see his daughter.

Connie had taken a few days' holiday time that was due to her to enable her to go with Sam to the race. Her parents were concerned about her going and staying overnight, until Sam called on them.

'Thank you so much for letting Connie come with us,' he said. 'She's part of the team now, a mascot, and we couldn't possibly go without her.' He looked at George. 'Don't worry, sir; I'll take good care of her, as will my two men. She'll be perfectly safe with us.'

'And where will she be sleeping?' Madge

asked sharply.

Connie was mortified, but her father stepped in.

'That's enough from you, Mother, thank you!' He shook Sam's hand. 'Good luck, young man. Take care on the track.'

Early on the following Saturday morning, Harry and Tom piled into the truck carrying the Riley and took off, closely followed by Sam and Connie on his motorcycle. It was a warm summer day and the weather forecast was good. They had all been praying for a dry track. Sam had explained how much more difficult it was when it was raining.

'Sometimes you can't see in front of you from the spray from the other cars, and that can be really frightening.'

She had pushed such a thought from her mind. She was worried enough about his safety as it was.

Although it was early when they arrived at Silverstone, it was already buzzing. Trucks of all sizes were arriving with the race vehicles. Spectators were gathering early to make sure of a good viewing position. Marshals were wandering around doing their jobs; mechanics were attending to their own particular vehicle like mother hens around a favourite child. Officials were inspecting each car, making sure it adhered to the conditions of the entry.

Sam happened to glance up as Jake and his men drove in. Sam told his mechanics, and they watched as the Jaguar was unloaded.

Jake saw them watching and grinned to himself. Well, here it is, Knight, he thought. This is my revenge for all the other races where you beat me. Today is mine!

Connie was on edge. This race was different, she could tell. There was a charged atmosphere all around her. It was one long race. Twenty laps of the course, and there were more cars entered this time. She could feel her heart thumping as the day wore on and the time for the start drew near. Sam and his mates were no longer jovial, they were there to win, and that was paramount in their minds. This was not the time for frivolity.

As the start grew nigh, Sam gathered Connie into his arms. 'Give me a hug,' he said. 'Now, I don't want you to worry, I'll be fine. We'll celebrate together tonight.' He kissed her hard and long.

Eventually, the cars were to be driven on the track. Each taking their place on the grid, according to their place on the race winner's table. Connie saw Jake was much further back than Sam, who was four cars from the front. She tucked her arm through Tom's for comfort.

He glanced down at her and saw the concern on her face. 'You have got to learn to relax, Connie, or you'll be a basket case by the end!'

'Don't tell me *you* feel relaxed,' she retorted, 'I can feel the tension in you just holding your arm!' They both laughed, which helped to relieve their feelings a little.

The drivers began revving their engines as the marshal stood holding the flag aloft. It dropped, and they were off!

Sam moved off quickly, threading his way through two cars in front of him, leaving Barton in his wake. Connie cheered loudly. She found herself stiffen when the car was out of sight on the other side of the track, but breathed a sigh of relief when Sam sped past the grandstand in third place.

To Connie, the race seemed endless and nerve-racking. As the race progressed, the lead cars changed place. At one time Sam had dropped back two places with Barton moving up.

As they drove past on the penultimate lap, Sam was behind the lead car. Connie and the two men could hardly contain their excitement, but they gasped aloud as they saw Jake try and overtake at speed, catching the rear of the car in front. They both spun out. Bits of metal flew over the track, and a wheel bounced over a fence, missing spectators by a miracle. The Jaguar piled into a load of hay bales and stopped, smoke pouring from beneath the bonnet. Everyone held their breath as Barton clambered out just before the vehicle erupted into flames. The other car stopped ahead of him but not close enough to be in danger from the flames. The driver ran over to Barton waving his fists angrily as marshals put out the fire with extinguishers. Stewards pulled the two drivers apart – as blows were exchanged – and led them away.

The race had to be stopped. There was debris on the track which was deemed too dangerous for the race to continue. The result was announced eventually, placing the cars in order they were in before the accident.

Sam stood on the rostrum in second place.

As Connie, Tom and Harry stood applauding, Tom tried to conceal his anger.

'If that bloody lunatic hadn't driven so dangerously, Sam stood a good chance of winning this race,' he declared.

'But hopefully no one was seriously hurt,' Connie said. She was just relieved the whole thing was over and that Sam was in one piece.

Back in the pits, Jake Barton was raging. He loudly blamed the other driver for the accident. 'If he hadn't moved over I could have caught up with Knight!'

His two mechanics had reached the end of their tethers. Charlie faced Barton and, grabbing him by the front of his overalls, he peered into his face, puce with anger.

'It was your bloody fault, Jake. You drove into the back of him in your haste to get past. You had no room for such a manoeuvre, and you know it! The car's a write-off, all because of your obsession. All our hard work for nothing!' He pushed the man away from him. 'Well, from here on in, you're on your own. Bert and me are leaving!'

'What do you mean, you're leaving?'

'We'll find work for another driver, one who wants to win races,' Bert said. 'A professional, not some fucking madman!'

The two men walked away leaving Barton speechless.

After the prize-giving, Sam saw his car safely loaded. He removed his overalls, took Connie by the hand and walked her to his motorcycle. 'It's time to celebrate, sweetheart,' he said and kissed her.

Eight

John Baker watched as Sam drove away with Connie on the pillion of his motorcycle. Having watched the race, he had to admit the man was a superb driver, but he couldn't help the feeling of jealousy as he thought this weekend would have been the perfect opportunity for him to take Connie to some hotel room and enjoy her young firm body. He couldn't help but wonder if that was where the two of them were heading now – to some discreet place to make love. He climbed into his car and joined the queue forming to leave the racetrack.

Sam drove as far as Banbury before stopping at a small country hotel, and as he climbed off the bike and removed his helmet, Connie saw how tired he looked. Why wouldn't he be, she thought. After all, the race was not only a long one, but the concentration he had needed was mentally draining too.

'Why don't we grab something to eat, and then I think you should sleep, you look worn out,' she said.

His look of relief was her reward. 'You really wouldn't mind?'

'No, of course not, why would I?'

Putting his arm round her he kissed her forehead. 'I promised we'd celebrate, that's why.'

'We can do that later. Come on, I could eat a horse!'

Although Sam was bone weary, he too was hungry, and they both ordered roast beef with all the trimmings. He was thirsty and ordered a pint beer at the bar, where they sat until they were called to the table. Connie had half a bitter. The fumes from the cars and the excitement of the race had dried her mouth too.

'Today was quite an education,' she told him. 'Very different from the last time I watched you race.'

He frowned. 'Yes, and if it hadn't been for that crazy bugger I'd have won it!'

'It was a miracle that no one was killed,' she said. 'When that wheel flew through the air I was certain someone was going to be hurt – or worse.'

Shaking his head, Sam said, 'I'll be very surprised if Barton isn't banned after today. He deliberately hit that car trying to pass when he didn't have the room. I suppose he thought he could shunt it out of the way. The man's a menace!'

Chuckling, she said, 'The other driver thumped Jake. The stewards had to pull them apart.'

At that moment they were told their table was ready and they settled down to eat.

Back at Silverstone, the race committee had summoned Jake Barton to their office and asked him to wait outside. Inside they discussed the accident and deliberated their next move. They were all in agreement that this time Barton, who was a rogue driver anyway, had gone too far and had deliberately endangered life. Some spectators had been injured, but fortunately there were no fatalities. His actions would not be tolerated. They called him in.

Half an hour later, he walked out of the office, his face white with shock. He wandered over to where the remains of the Jaguar were being loaded on to his truck and stood looking at the wreck as he smoked a cigarette and tried to come to terms with the decision made against him. He'd been banned from racing for six months, his mechanics had walked out and now he was on his own. He couldn't believe it. He still had his garage where he worked on private cars, but that wasn't who he was. He was a racing driver first and foremost. They couldn't do this to him! Well, he'd appeal. No way could he allow Sam Knight to have a clear field. No way!

Connie and Sam had finished eating and had made their way to their room. Connie went into the bathroom to freshen up, and when she returned Sam was lying on the bed asleep, fully dressed. She gazed fondly at him and carefully removed his shoes, then climbed on the bed beside him, where she too fell asleep, the excitement of the day catching up with her also.

Several hours later she woke. The bed next to her was empty, and she could hear the bathwater running. Stretching her stiff legs, she climbed off the bed, looked at her watch and was surprised to see it was eight o'clock. Sitting in front of the dressing table, she combed her tussled hair, freshened her make-up and waited. Her heart beating a little faster as she did so.

In a few minutes, Sam came out of the bathroom wearing just a bath towel around his waist. He smiled at her when he saw she was awake.

'Feel better now?' he asked as he leaned over and kissed her.

'I can't believe I slept so long.'

He pulled her to her feet and held her close. 'We both needed to rest, but now...'

As he put his arms around her, she could smell the scent of soap and aftershave, feel the taut body against hers. Felt the longing in her loins as he kissed and caressed her.

Sam slowly undressed her and led her to

the bed. He was a considerate lover, making sure she was enjoying every move, whispering words of love in her ear as he explored her body endlessly with fingers that caressed and probed until she thought she'd die with longing, and when he eventually entered her, she was ready for him.

At last they lay exhausted in each other's arms. Replete, content. He held her close, stroking her face, kissing her. Running his fingers through her hair.

Connie lay beside him, marvelling at the warmth of his body. This wasn't like the sex she'd had with John Baker. This was different. There was a tenderness about it, a meaning. It wasn't just sex for sex's sake, and she realized how she'd let herself be used before. But with Sam she'd felt special. Cosseted ... loved, even. She gazed up at him and thought how lucky she was.

He looked back at her with affection, but there was something else she couldn't fathom. Puzzlement? Then the realization came. Had he guessed after all that she wasn't the virgin he'd imagined her to be? She didn't dare put her fears into words, but waited to see if he said anything. But the moment passed, and he said nothing. She breathed a sigh of relief.

'Come on,' he said. 'Let's get dressed and go down to the bar for a drink. Are you hungry?'

'Not really after such a big lunch, just peckish.'

'Me too, we'll order some sandwiches.'

The bar was busy, and they knew from the conversation that there were some spectators from the race meeting there. They were discussing the accident. Sam and Connie sat quietly and listened.

'That Jake Barton is a madman,' said one. 'I've seen him race before, he has no consideration for other drivers, he's just hell-bent on winning.'

'Well, he won't be doing that for a while,' said another. 'I heard the committee has banned him for six months.'

'And so they should! People were injured out there today, all because of him.'

Connie looked quickly at Sam, who put his finger to his lips. He hoped no one would recognize him in the crowded bar.

'Damned shame!' remarked another man. 'That Sam Knight had the race in the palm of his hand, as far as I'm concerned. I reckon he'd have won but for Barton.'

They all agreed. 'I also heard that Barton has a bee in his bonnet about Knight. He thinks he's the better driver and he was trying to catch him when he crashed.'

'He's not in the same class as Sam Knight,' said the first man. 'Now there is a good driver!'

Connie was thrilled to hear this. After all

she was with Sam and he'd just made love to her. She swelled with pride, but Sam turned away so the men couldn't see his face. The last thing he wanted was to be involved in this conversation and was relieved when the men left the bar together and he could relax.

'So Barton's been given a six-month ban. He's lucky not to be banned forever,' he remarked. 'To be honest I'm not surprised, and racing will be that much safer without him.'

'From what you and the boys have said, he won't be happy about that, will he?' asked Connie.

'Oh, no! I expect he'll appeal. But I doubt he'll win. He's been pushing his luck for a very long time. He's been warned before now.'

Connie didn't say any more but the whole scenario worried her. She'd seen Jake Barton at the track and thought he looked a nasty piece of work.

The next morning Connie and Sam made love again, then reluctantly left their room to have breakfast before driving home. She'd loved every moment with him and told him so.

'I'm glad,' he said. 'My way of life doesn't suit everyone, but it's who I am and it will be this way for many years to come, I hope. Next month at Brands Hatch there is a Formula One race and I'm going to take you to see it. That's for real drivers!'

'But you're a real driver!'

He laughed. 'Yes, in Touring Car Racing, but these are the big boys. You've not seen anything until you see Stirling Moss and Juan Manuel Fangio behind a wheel. Their cars are real beasts.'

'Do you want to be like them?' She didn't like the sound of this at all.

'It would be wonderful, but frankly, I think I'm where I belong.'

The following day the local paper was full of the race and casualties. Barton's picture blazed across the front page. LOCAL DRIVER CAUSES CRASH AT SILVER-STONE. The following report ended by saying he was now banned for only six months when some thought the ban should have been permanent.

When Jake read the report he went ber-serk. Alone in his garage, he picked up a spanner and hurled it into space, then strode around cursing loudly. He felt no remorse for the damage he'd caused but was filled only with outrage at what he saw as an injustice from the committee towards him. They couldn't put an end to his racing, he wouldn't allow it! Surely they would see sense at the appeal when the furore had died down. Having convinced himself of this he went to the pub.

As soon as he walked in, the chatter ceased and he felt everyone looking at him, but only the landlord spoke.

'Usual, Jake?'

Jake nodded, paid for his beer and sat down, aware that he was the main topic of conversation, albeit in low tones. He was never a man to take criticism, and eventually he got to his feet.

'All right, you bastards! If you've got something to say, say it to my face!' He looked at them defiantly.

There was a lot of mumbling by those who knew of his volatile nature, but there was one brave man among them. 'It's about bloody time you were taken off the racetrack! I've seen you race, and you're a danger to everyone – including yourself.'

'What gives you the right to say that?'

'I was at the meeting yesterday, standing close by where you crashed. There was no way you could have passed that car safely but you didn't give a toss. A piece of your car nearly took my head off! That's what gives me the right, mate! As far as I'm concerned you should never be allowed on a track ever again!'

There were mutters of approval from the others.

Then the man added, 'Pity you don't drive like Sam Knight! At least he doesn't put other drivers at risk, and he manages to win races. You should take a page out of his book!'

It was the last thing he should have said to Jake Barton. Jake flew at him and punched him in the jaw, but the landlord jumped the counter and dragged him away. Then pushing him to the door he said, 'You're barred, Jake. I don't want you in here ever again!' Then he shoved him outside and slammed the door in his face.

Barton was livid and kicked the door, yelling expletives.

'That's enough of that, now; stop it or I'll take you down to the station for disturbing the peace and damaging private property!'

Spinning round, Jake saw a police constable standing before him.

Seeing the anger in the other man's eyes, the policeman continued, 'Don't be foolish, Mr Barton. You're in enough trouble, I would have thought. Go home!'

Jake knew it was time to leave. If he was to win his appeal he couldn't be in trouble with the law. He reluctantly walked away.

Nine

In the store on the Monday, Connie told Betty she'd been to watch the race at Silverstone and she told her about the accident. She didn't, however, tell her she'd stayed the night with Sam. She didn't want her friend's disapproval to spoil it all.

Several times during the morning, as she served her customers, she noticed John Baker watching her from a distance. It surprised her as he'd kept well out of her way after their last confrontation ... and she wondered why he was doing it. When Betty left the counter for her lunch break, he wandered over.

'Enjoy your weekend, Connie?'

She was mystified at the interest. 'Yes, thank you.'

'Your boyfriend's a good driver, I'll give him that.'

She looked at him in astonishment.

'I was at Silverstone and watched the race. After, I saw you leave on the back of his bike.'

Connie remained silent, wondering where this conversation was going.

Baker's gaze shifted to her bosom and back again. 'Take you to bed, did he, after the meeting?'

She felt the colour rise in her cheeks, both from embarrassment and outrage. 'What I do and with whom is not any of your business,' she snapped, keeping her voice low.

'Have you told him about our affair? How we would meet after work, what we got up to, how we spent a weekend in Bournemouth?' Seeing the anxious expression in her eyes, he continued, 'Don't tell me he thinks you're still a virgin? Oh my, is he in for a surprise!'

'What ever do you mean?' Now she was worried, as she'd learned her ex-lover could be quite vicious when he wanted to be.

'If you want to find out, you'd better meet me in the park after work. Usual place.'

She watched him walk away. What was she to do? What did he mean? There was a definite threat behind his words, and now he knew Sam by sight. Would he tell him about their relationship, would he be that mean and spoil everything for her? She was beside herself with worry. If John did tell Sam he'd had sex with her, would Sam ever want to see her again? Her mind was in turmoil. *Oh my God, I can't let that happen,* she thought. *I'll have to meet him and find out what's on his mind.*

For his part, John Baker was more than pleased with Connie's reaction. He knew he had her worried; now she would be at his mercy. He gave a sly smile. She would have no choice but to do his bidding – and he had definite plans for her.

After closing time, Connie put on her jacket and left the store, walking slowly to the park, her heart beating wildly as she neared the rockery. Her whole future could be at risk during her meeting with Baker, and she was nervous, but she vowed not to let him see this.

John was sitting on a bench, smoking a cigarette, and as he saw her approach he rose to his feet. 'There you are. Come and sit down, we have something to discuss.'

As Connie sat beside him she glared at him. 'As far as I'm concerned, there's nothing left to say.'

'Then why did you come and meet me?'

'Because I didn't like you trying to threaten me, that's why. I'm here to tell you to back off! Leave me alone. You've managed to do that for some time without any problem and that's the way I want it to stay!'

He ran his finger down her cheek. 'I love it when you're angry, your nostrils flare. I find it very sexy.'

She pushed his hand away. 'What do you want, John?'

'Oh, Connie, I love that about you, you're always so direct.' He studied every feature of her face slowly then he smiled. 'I want *you*, darling.'

'You what?' She could scarcely believe what she'd heard.

He ignored her outburst. 'As you know, Kay and I have parted, and now I have a flat in the Polygon area. It will be so much easier for us to be together. It will be our little love nest ... and nobody need know.'

Connie was appalled. 'You must be joking!'

The smile disappeared. 'I have never been more serious in my life! If you want your boyfriend kept in the dark about us, you'll do as I ask.'

'That's blackmail!'

'I'm afraid it is, darling, but think how good we were together, how much you ached for me to touch you – to love you. Remember? Because I do.' He grabbed her wrist. 'Now we can enjoy it all again, and your boyfriend need never know, it'll be our little secret.'

She looked at him and wondered however she could have found this man so attractive, because now all she felt for him was hatred. The sophistication, the charm had all been stripped away, and she saw a conniving, lecherous creep, a man who would stoop to anything to get his way.

Connie stood up; flushed with anger, she cast a look of utter disdain at him. 'What's the matter, John? No woman to pleasure your bed? That's not like you, you usually have somebody lined up ready for when you got bored. At least that was what I heard

118

when first I joined the staff.'

She saw the anger in his face. 'Oh yes, your reputation is well-known at the store, yet I fell for your charm just that same. You took advantage of a young girl.'

'I made you a woman!' he retorted.

She grinned at him. 'Yes, you did, and you were a good lover – but then you'd had so much practice, hadn't you?'

'Your boyfriend will be very disappointed when I tell him what you are really like, not the little innocent he believes you to be.'

Connie stood tall and stared at him. 'Don't threaten me, John, because if you continue to do so, I'll go to the managing director at Tyrell's and tell him you keep bothering me for sex! Not the kind of thing they want to hear about a floor manager. You could lose your job!'

'If you did, it would be your word against mine.'

'True, but they must be aware of your reputation, after all it's hardly a secret, and they would have to take my accusation seriously. Your job would certainly be in jeopardy. So you'd better think about that!' She turned on her heel and left him, her legs shaking beneath her, praying they'd at least carry her safely out of his sight before they gave way.

Connie made it to a nearby cafe, sank gratefully into a chair and ordered a pot of tea to give her time to recover. She poured the tea when it was served and picked up the cup with both hands, to stop the tremble in them, and sipped the comforting brew, praying her bluff had done the trick – that John'd be scared off. Sam was important to her, and she couldn't bear the fact that their new relationship could be marred by such a man.

Kay found it easier than she thought to be without her husband. After so many years of wondering if he was with another woman, she no longer cared, and it had given her a sense of freedom. Indeed her routine was very different. She had only Susan to consider now, which was no hardship; her washing and ironing load had halved, as John had been most fastidious about his clothing; and she had more time on her hands. She decided this was a fresh start and set about making changes. She started with herself first.

At the hairdressers she had her hair cut into a new style after reading about the new whizz kid hairdresser, Vidal Sassoon, who was all the rage at the moment, and she had blonde streaks put in her chestnut hair. The girl at the beauty counter helped her choose different make-up and sat her in front of a mirror and made up her face, showing her how to use the rouge and eyeshadow to highlight her good points. She then went to a gown shop and bought two dresses and, afterwards, a pair of shoes.

That evening, when Susan was in bed, she had a bath and tried on her new finery, turning back and forth in front of a full-length mirror. She was tall with a trim figure and both dresses showed her curves and the court shoes her shapely legs. Patting her new hairstyle in place, she was delighted at the reflection.

'You don't know what you're missing, John,' she said and laughed. She was still a young woman. There was still time for her to enjoy another man. But she doubted she'd marry again. With a young child that wouldn't be easy, but a lover now that would be interesting. Perhaps she'd see just what it was about it that had seemed to thrill her husband so much. But where to meet such a person? Obviously, she couldn't go dancing unless she had a babysitter, and who would she go with? All her old friends were married. Perhaps she'd get a part-time job to fit in with Susan's school hours. At least that would get her out of the house, mixing with people. She'd buy the local paper and look in the situations vacant to see what was on offer.

At that moment her front doorbell rang. Still in her finery, she went downstairs to open the door. To her surprise her neighbour Rob was standing there.

He looked her up and down, appreciating the attractive woman before him.

'Hello, Rob, what can I do for you?'

'Barbara's out with her friends and I forgot to bring some milk home. Don't suppose you have any to spare, do you?'

'Come along in,' she said, 'as it happens I do have a spare pint you can have.'

He followed her into the kitchen. 'I must say, Kay, you're looking very fetching this evening. New outfit?'

Opening the fridge door she said, 'As a matter of fact, it is. I bought it today.'

'Very nice. Really shows off your figure. Look, I don't mean to be personal, but I heard about you and John splitting up, and I'm sorry.'

'Yes, well, you know, these things happen.' She was a little embarrassed. She'd only told a few people, and it still made her uncomfortable if it was mentioned.

'The man's crazy! Look at you, good heavens, couldn't he see what he was losing?'

'I'd rather not talk about it, Rob, if you don't mind.'

He took a step towards her and placed a hand on her shoulder. Softly he said, 'If you ever feel that you want the comfort of a man, just let me know. I'd be only too happy to oblige.'

She looked at him with astonishment and anger. 'How dare you! You have a perfectly lovely wife at home, and whatever makes you think I'd even consider such a thing?' She didn't give him chance to answer. 'You are no better than the man I've just got rid of. Get out of my house ... now!'

'Sorry, sorry! I didn't mean to offend you, Kay.'

'Out! And don't ever come round here on some pretence again. In fact just don't come round!' She walked to the front door and opened it.

Looking somewhat crestfallen he walked past her and turned, about to say something, but the glare Kay gave him stopped him – and he left.

She walked back into her kitchen fuming. Men! They were all the bloody same, couldn't keep their brains above their trouser belts. Then she started to laugh. At least she was still attractive to men – even if they were undesirable. Poor Barbara, she'd be so upset if she knew her husband had just propositioned her. Of course, she'd never tell her. She didn't want to be the one to spoil another marriage, and once you lost trust in your husband life was never the same, she knew that well enough.

For his part, her neighbour Rob was smarting from the rejection. He'd never been unfaithful to his wife but he'd always had a hankering for the lovely Kay and indeed had been envious of John having such an attractive woman to share his bed. Not that there was anything wrong with Barbara, his own wife. She was pretty enough, but Kay had something about her – a sexual aura – and he'd fantasized about the two of them together. Today had been the first opportunity to perhaps make it a reality. He shrugged. Perhaps it was too soon to make himself available to her. Maybe after some time had passed she'd feel lonely, and then he would make sure he was around. But as he made a pot of tea he realized he still didn't have any milk and cursed.

The following weekend Sam took Connie to see 'the big boys' at Silverstone, as promised. He pointed out the renowned drivers, Stirling Moss, Juan Fangio, and others. People she'd only ever seen on newsreels in the cinema and in the newspapers. It was all very exciting. But as she watched the race, she was greatly relieved that Sam was in touring cars. The speeds that these cars reached made her hair stand on end! She wondered just why men were so in love with racing cars; it was fraught with danger.

The race was eventually won by Fangio, driving an Alfa Romeo, with Moss in second place. When it was over, Connie's body was stiff with tension, and when they stopped for a bite to eat, she voiced her concerns to Sam.

'I thought touring car racing was hazardous, but today was crazy! Doesn't anyone get killed at these speeds?'

'Sadly they do,' he told her.

Her eyes widened with horror! 'Then what on earth are you doing in such a dangerous sport?'

He gave a wry smile. 'You might ask the same of a mountaineer or a test pilot. There's something in the blood that drives you on.' He tried to lessen her concerns. 'I'm not saying there is no danger in touring cars, of course there is. Anything to do with speed has its dangers, but as you saw today, these car engines are much bigger and so they are capable of higher speeds. I have no ambition to be a Formula One driver, Connie. I'm happy where I am.'

She gazed at him as he tried to reassure her and realized this young man meant a great deal to her. She didn't want to lose him either because of his motor sport or because he might find out about her and John Baker. The first, an honourable thing, the second, a more tawdry reason.

'You just make sure you keep safe then!' she said and squeezed his hand.

Laughing he said, 'You won't get rid of me that easily!'

Under the table she crossed her fingers and silently prayed that he was right.

Ten

Jake Barton was finding life more than difficult. No longer able to race and now minus his two good mechanics, he'd had to change course in business. He hired another man and was now running his garage, repairing cars. He bought one at an auction for a small amount of cash and was rebuilding it ready to respray and sell on. He wasn't a bad mechanic when he set his mind to it, and now he needed to make money to keep him afloat. But, all the time, he still blamed Sam for his misfortune. The fact that his rival had won a couple more races didn't sit well with him, but he had to get on with his way of life until he came up with another way to make money.

Jake had no friends. He was a difficult man and others kept away from him and his volatile temper. Because of this, Jake had moved to another area in the docks to do his drinking. He'd had no choice really, having been barred from his usual pub. The only thing he was exceptionally good at was playing darts, which he did at his new local. This at least allowed him to be sociable with other men, without animosity, and it was whilst he was playing with another customer that the opportunity to make money came his way.

Gerry Cooper, a small-time crook, enjoyed a game of darts during his leisure hours and, being bloody minded himself, felt a certain camaraderie with Barton. They both spoke the same kind of language. Gerry knew about Jake losing his racing licence and had taken the trouble to look into his business, realizing that things were not going well. After a game of darts, the two men sat down to enjoy a glass of beer paid for by Gerry, the loser, as was the custom.

'I expect things are a bit quiet for you these days,' Gerry ventured.

Jake's expression darkened. 'What's it to you?'

Ignoring the outburst, Gerry said, 'Well, I might be able to put something your way which would make you a bit of dosh ... as long as you can keep your mouth shut!'

A look of interest dispelled the one of anger and Jake asked, 'Really? And what might that be?'

Gerry leaned forward and spoke quietly. 'Well, it's like this...'

Christmas was approaching. Tyrell and Greens was beautifully decorated throughout the store and business was brisk. Connie's threat to John Baker, it seemed, had worked, as he kept his distance these days, which was a great relief to her. It solved her problem of keeping their relationship a secret from Sam.

Her family now accepted Sam as her boyfriend, and he and her father became firm friends when Sam invited him to accompany Connie to a race meeting one weekend. George Morgan was very impressed with what he saw and was cheering Sam loudly during the final laps of the race as he finally drove over the finishing line, the winner. The older man was full of admiration for the young man, which thrilled Connie, of course.

The final race of the year was over, and now Sam and Connie were able to spend more time together. Sam had a small one bedroom flat in Henstead Court where Connie spent many an evening and occasionally a weekend. She had been quite open about this with her mother, Dorothy, who at first had tried to talk about the dangers to a young girl in this situation.

'What happens if you get pregnant?'

'I won't, I promise. We are very careful to take precautions, Mum.'

Dorothy was embarrassed to be given so much information. 'You are my baby,' she retorted, 'I don't find it easy to think of you in bed with a man you're not married to!'

'Mum, I'm twenty now, I'm not a child!'

Dorothy reached out and placed a hand on her daughter's shoulder. 'I know, but even when you are middle aged, you'll still be my child. When you have a family of your own, you'll understand.' She hesitated. 'Has Sam ever mentioned marriage?'

Connie blushed. 'We've skirted around the subject. I know Sam loves me, he's told me so, and I know from the way he talks that he sees our future together. He's always talking about what we'll be doing next year … and I love him, Mum.'

Her mother put her arms around her. 'Just take care. I don't want to see you get hurt, that's all.'

Dorothy had broached the subject when in bed with George, but he wasn't worried.

'At least she's honest about it instead of lying to us. Sam Knight is a regular bloke. I like him; he has principles. I know he loves our girl; it's obvious when you see them together. He'll take good care of her, don't you fret, and I'm sure one day I'll be giving her away to him as a bride.'

Madge, Connie's grandmother, had different ideas, which she voiced loudly one afternoon as she watched Dorothy work her way through a pile of ironing, much of which belonged to Madge herself.

'I suppose Connie will be away this weekend again!'

Dorothy just looked at her and carried on.

'Not surprised you don't want to talk about it, her staying with that man and not being even engaged! Well, I'm at a loss for words, the way you let her behave!'

Folding a petticoat of Madge's, Dorothy raised her eyebrows. 'You, at a loss for words? Well, that would be a first!'

'There's no need to be rude. *My* daughter wasn't allowed to behave in such a manner, I can tell you!'

'No, you're right. You tried to tie her down so much she left home, as I recall!'

'She found a job in a different town, that's why,' Madge retorted.

Dorothy put down her iron and glared at her mother-in-law. 'That's what you tell yourself, but you know she did that to get away from you because you were such a bitch to her!'

Madge's mouth fell open with surprise.

'You know, sometimes I feel really sorry for you. You must be a desperately unhappy woman to behave the way you do. You never have a good word to say about anyone. You have no idea the amount of pleasure you've missed in life because of it.' She picked up the iron. 'Now if you want me to finish ironing all your clothes, you could get up and make us a pot of tea for once!'

Madge was so shaken by this sudden verbal attack from her daughter-in-law, she rose from the chair without another word.

Dorothy watched her walk into the kitchen and smiled mischievously. It gave her a perverse pleasure to take a rise out of the old woman sometimes. It certainly helped her to cope with the feelings of resentment that were always smouldering just below the surface. They say everyone has a cross to bear in life, and Madge was hers.

On Saturday, at the close of business, Sam was waiting outside the staff entrance for Connie, seated in his Riley, when a stranger walked around the car, inspecting it with interest. He then walked to the driver's side and, as Sam wound down the window, he spoke.

'Nice car. I saw you race this earlier this year at Silverstone. It was the day of the accident on the track. I was sure the race was yours until that happened.'

Sam climbed out of the car. 'Nice of you to say so, and I thought the race was mine too, but there you go. Nothing is certain in this life, is it?'

The man laughed. 'You couldn't have said a truer word.'

At that moment Connie walked out of the door, saw the car and froze. Sam was in deep conversation with John Baker. For one moment she felt faint and clasped at the nearby wall, watching them. They seemed to be having a cheerful conversation as they both were smiling. Taking a deep breath she walked towards them.

Sam saw her first. 'Hello, sweetheart, this gentleman was telling me he'd seen me race at Silverstone. We've been discussing cars.'

'Hello, Connie,' said Baker.

'Oh, you two know each other then?'

'This is Mr Baker, my floor manager,' Connie informed him coldly. 'Are you ready to go?'

'I won't keep you any longer, Mr Knight,' said John with a smile. 'It was nice talking to you.' He looked at Connie, his eyes glittering, his smile betraying his true feelings. 'Have a nice weekend.'

Connie climbed hastily into the passenger seat.

'Seems a decent chap,' Sam remarked as he started the engine.

'When he wants to be,' she answered somewhat tartly.

As they drove past her ex-lover he just stared at her, his face set in grim lines. There was no smile now.

Connie felt her stomach tighten as they drove away. What was John's game? He'd left her alone for so long that she thought she had made him back off, but now... She could feel the tension in her body as she fretted about the situation.

The tension was still there as later, in bed,

Sam took her into his arms and kissed her. He looked puzzled. 'Hey! What's the matter? You're tighter than a spring.'

'It's just been such a hectic day in the store,' she lied. 'You know, the pre-Christmas rush.'

'Well, we'll have to see what I can do about that.'

But no matter how he tried, he couldn't release the tension, and eventually Connie pushed him gently away. 'I'm sorry; I guess I'm just not in the mood.'

Sam chuckled softly. 'You don't have a headache, I suppose?'

She saw the humour and smiled. 'No, I don't, I'm just weary, that's all.'

He lay back on his pillow, one arm around her. 'It's that bloke, isn't it?'

'What?'

'Well, ever since you saw me talking to your manager you've been different. You closed up. It was like sitting beside an ice cube. What is it about him that makes you feel like that?'

Connie was startled. She had to choose her words carefully now or this conversation could become dangerous.

'I just don't like him. He's not an easy man to work for. He can be very demanding, and he has made my life difficult sometimes if he's thought I've not been doing something right. Tonight he was trying to be charming. It didn't wash with me, that's all.'

'Oh, I see. Well, that's understandable. But you know, Connie, in the workplace you have to do your job, which means you don't always make friends.'

'Are you defending him?' She was angry.

'Hey! Steady, I'm on your side, sweetheart, always. Just making an observation.'

She snuggled into him. 'I don't want to talk about him, all right?'

He cuddled her and laughed. 'I get the message. Now, go to sleep, perhaps you'll feel better in the morning.'

During the Sunday, Connie tried to keep her thoughts of Baker at bay. She played her part well, and they enjoyed lunch out by the Hamble River and the drive through the surrounding country before returning to the flat, sitting in front of the small television Sam had rented, until it was time for bed. This time she was relaxed enough to respond to his love-making, but as she lay in his arms after, listening to his soft breathing as he slept, she wondered just what was waiting for her on the morrow, back in the store. John Baker had surfaced again, and that meant danger to her relationship with Sam.

On Monday morning, Sam drove Connie to work. 'I don't know what's on this week at the garage,' he said. 'I have a car coming in this morning, and it needs a lot of work done on it. When I'm free, I'll either meet you from work or call round and let you know.' He kissed her goodbye and opened the car door for her.

Connie hung up her coat, combed her hair and entered the store. She and Betty tidied their goods, dusting the display ready for the first customer. She saw John across the department floor watching her.

At the end of the day, Connie walked through the staff door with a sigh of relief. But as she turned the corner, Baker, hidden in the dark, grabbed her arm and pulled her to him.

'Nice chap, your boyfriend. The trusting type, I would think.'

'Don't start that all over again!' she retorted.

He laughed. 'I got my divorce papers today. My wife is suing me for adultery. She's named you as correspondent!'

'What?' Connie suddenly felt nauseous.

'What do you think your boyfriend will think of that? All local divorces are written up in the *Echo*. He won't like that. His friends will taunt him about it no doubt when they read about it. His sweet innocent lady friend, named and shamed.'

'What proof has she?' demanded Connie. 'She can't name anyone without proof!'

He shrugged. 'Maybe she found out about us going to Bournemouth. We were registered as Mr and Mrs Baker, after all.'

She glared at him. 'You're loving this, aren't you? You can't bear to think of me in the arms of another man. A much better man than you will ever be!'

He was outraged.

She cried out as John grasped her by the shoulders, his fingers digging into her through her coat. 'Is he better in bed than me? Does he make you beg him to take you – as I did?'

Her rage knew no bounds. 'Yes, and yes again! He's a wonderful lover, and he really loves me! He doesn't just want me for sex like you did.'

His cruel laugh echoed. 'That's what all men say to get what they want. I said it to you, and you believed me.'

Connie tried to calm down. 'I was younger then, but I've learned to tell between lies and the truth. You see, I trust Sam. I never really trusted you.'

'Then why did you meet me so often and come to Bournemouth with me?'

'Oh, to begin with I was flattered. I enjoyed being kissed and made a fuss of, and I planned to lose my virginity and you happened to be around at the time.'

He looked at her with astonishment. 'You are very calculating, Connie, which I must say surprises me.'

'Well, John, you made me grow up rather quickly, and I suppose I should thank you for that. You taught me all I know about sex. You were a good teacher. In that, I was lucky; it could have been someone who wasn't so well practised in seduction.'

He was at a loss as to how to handle this change in his former lover. 'You have changed almost beyond recognition,' was his only comment.

'No. Just grown up. Don't think for one moment what you've told me about your divorce will change things between us, John. I won't be unfaithful to Sam, no matter what you try and throw at me. But be very careful, because I could destroy you if I had a mind to.'

As she walked away, she hoped that now he would stop interfering in her life, but the news of his divorce had shaken her. The only concrete proof his wife could have of her being part of her husband's infidelity was if she'd discovered their stay in Bournemouth. How could she possibly know about that? Was he bluffing? If he wasn't and it all came out in the local press, what affect would it have on Sam? Should she confess to him about her relationship with John Baker or wait? She didn't know what to do for the best.

Eleven

Unaware of the chaos her divorce papers were causing her ex-husband, Kay Baker had taken control of her new life. Susan was now attending nursery school all day, and Kay had secured a part-time job in an office, thankful she'd kept up her typing skills at home. With the maintenance being paid by John for his daughter and the mortgage covered by him – for the moment – the extra money she earned paid for the treats.

Now that she had a job, she was beginning to have a social life. The office of one of the council departments in the Civic Centre was a busy place, dealing with the paperwork required by various divisions incurring works on public and council buildings. It was interesting, and her colleagues were a friendly bunch. A Christmas party was looming, and Kay had been persuaded to go and let Susan sleep over at her grandmother's house for the Saturday evening. Her mother had been enthusiastic for Kay to start enjoying herself.

'Of course we'll have Susan,' she said when asked. 'It's time for you to get out and meet people socially. Find yourself a good man this time!'

'Oh, Mum! I'm just about to get my divorce, and believe me, I'm not looking for another husband just yet.'

'Who said anything about getting married?' said her mother archly.

Kay looked at her in surprise. 'What are you saying then?'

'Go and have some fun. Make sure the man takes precautions, that's all.'

Kay started to laugh. 'That's not what I expect my mother to say.'

Joan Thomas slowly sipped her tea. 'I've been married to your father for forty-two years. He's the only man I've ever known, in the biblical sense.'

Kay wondered what on earth was coming.

'I love him, you know I do, he's a dear, but sometimes I wonder just how it would have felt to be loved by someone else.'

'Mother!' Frowning, she asked, 'Are you sorry you married Dad?'

'Good heavens, no! But if I had my time over, I'd certainly have had a bit of fun before I settled down.'

'Good God, Mum, in your day you'd have been termed a loose woman.'

It was Joan's turn to laugh. 'Maybe, but I would have lived instead of wondering. Since the war, the laws of morality have changed. Sadly, I was born too soon.'

Kay looked askance at her mother. 'Just as well after what you've just been telling me.

Don't you start putting ideas into Susan's head when she's here!'

'As if I would! Anyway, by the time she grows up, it will have all changed again.'

The office party was being held at the Polygon Hotel. There was to be a reception, followed by dinner and dancing until midnight. Cocktail dresses and lounge suits were the order of the day. Kay had bought a brown chiffon dress with a swathed bodice, from a boutique in the town. It was fitted, low cut, with thin straps. She had looked at herself in the mirror of the dressing room in the shop and been thrilled at her reflection. Was it a bit too glamorous for an office do? Oh, what the hell, she thought – and paid the bill. Then she bought a pair of bronze evening shoes to wear with it and a light beige shawl, with a hint of gold sparkle, to wear around her shoulders.

On the night of the party, she stepped out of the taxi and entered the hotel, her heart beating wildly. This was her first proper outing since John had moved out, and she was distinctly nervous walking in alone. She entered the bar where the reception was held, pulling the shawl across her bosom, suddenly feeling somewhat naked.

Seeing two of her colleagues with whom she'd become very friendly at work, Kay walked over to them. At least with them she

140

felt at ease. They were standing with two gentlemen who they introduced as their husbands, but somehow they seemed less than friendly, which puzzled Kay, until one of them placed an arm possessively through her husband's. Then it dawned on her. She was now single, and these women saw her as a threat. It was a 'keep off the grass' sign, which Kay thought was insidious. She made her excuses and moved away.

The barman smiled and handed her a glass of champagne. Sitting on a bar stool, she gazed around the room, wishing she'd stayed at home. Taking out a cigarette she searched for her lighter. Beside her a gentleman lit his and held it out to her.

'Thank you,' she said as she looked up into the bluest eyes she'd ever seen.

'My pleasure.' The voice was low, cultured and mellifluous. The man was tall, well dressed in a navy suit, pale blue shirt and striped tie, with dark hair, slightly greying at the temples. She wondered who he was and what he was doing there. To her he was a complete stranger.

'Edward Harrington,' he said, holding out his hand.

Shaking it, she replied, 'Kay Baker.'

Glancing at her wedding ring he asked, 'Are you waiting for your husband, Mrs Baker?'

Shaking her head she said, 'No, Mr Harrington, I'm separated, waiting for a divorce, as it happens.'

'Then this is my lucky night.' His smile was inviting, and Kay felt a frisson of excitement as she looked at him.

'What brings you here tonight?' she enquired.

'Duty,' he said somewhat ruefully. 'I work for the department. To be honest I hate these affairs, however I have to make an appearance. And you?'

She explained where she worked. 'I was persuaded to come along. I think it was a big mistake.'

He chuckled. 'I saw you when you arrived and the way you were frozen out of that little group over there.' He nodded towards the foursome she'd approached earlier. 'Mind you, I'm not surprised – you look incredible.'

She felt her cheeks flush.

He ordered them both another glass of champagne. 'Now, Mrs Baker, how about we put aside our reluctance to be here and join forces? Together we could turn the whole thing around and enjoy ourselves. What do you say?'

Kay glanced across the room and saw her friends watching her with interest. 'Why not? I think it could be great fun.'

'Excellent!' He held up his glass. 'To a good night, Mrs Baker!'

Holding her glass up for the toast she said,

'In which case, call me Kay.'

'Lovely name ... I'm Edward.'

At that moment Kay's boss approached. 'Good evening, Mr Harrington,' he said. 'Would you like to join our table for dinner?'

His tone of deference surprised Kay. This man was usually overbearing and full of confidence.

'That's very thoughtful of you, James, but Mrs Baker and I have other plans. But thank you for your kindness. Don't let us keep you from your friends.'

Thus dismissed, the man walked away. Edward summoned the barman and asked to see the head waiter. When he arrived, Edward asked him to save a table for two in the dining room when dinner was served.

'Of course, sir. Is there anything else I can do for you?'

'Yes, there is.' Edward asked for a bottle of champagne to be put on ice and placed on the table.'

Kay was amused by the whole procedure. 'It would seem, Edward, that you are someone of importance, from the service you're getting here.'

He grinned at her. 'My position does afford me some privileges, I suppose. I try not to abuse it, but it does come in handy at times, I must confess.'

'Perhaps you should enlighten me before we dine?'

'Absolutely not! It would spoil the mystery. Let's just enjoy each other's company.'

At that moment the announcement came that dinner was served.

It gave Kay a perverse pleasure to be led into the dining room on the arm of such a handsome man. She smiled at her two colleagues as she passed them, trying not to appear triumphant.

The evening was a great success. Her companion was a good conversationalist and amusing, and after a sumptuous meal they danced the evening away. Kay was enjoying every moment, until midnight, when it ended.

'I feel a bit like Cinderella,' she said as they walked towards the reception. 'I must get the concierge to book me a taxi.'

'Nonsense! My driver will drop you off before he takes me home.' He led her outside towards a sleek car. The driver got out and held the door open.

'Thank you, Jake. Now, Kay, where do you live?'

It was Christmas Eve. In the town, the inhabitants, collars turned up against the cold, were dashing about with last-minute shopping. Butchers were hoping to sell the last of the turkeys, Christmas trees were being loaded on to cars, and Connie and the staff at Tyrell and Greens were rushed off their feet. At the close of day, she and Betty made their weary way to the staff room where they exchanged gifts before making their way home.

'What's Sam getting you, do you know?' Betty asked.

'I have no idea. I've bought him a jumper and some aftershave. He's coming to Christmas dinner and on Boxing Day, we are going to his parents for lunch.'

'Oh my! You've not met them yet, have you?'

'No,' said Connie with a grimace. 'I'm really nervous. They live in Poole, so we'll be driving there in the morning. There shouldn't be too much traffic on the road. Gosh, I hope they like me.'

Betty gave her a hug. 'Stop worrying, you'll be fine. Happy Christmas, Connie.'

'Same to you. See you in three days. Don't drink too much!'

On her way home, that Christmas Eve, Connie walked past all the shops with their brightly coloured windows, still full of festive gifts, knowing that immediately after the holiday the January sales would begin and life would be hectic in the preparation before – and then the sales themselves. But until then, she would enjoy the break. She only hoped that her grandmother would make the effort to be in a festive frame of mind.

She need not have worried. Her mother had been having the same thought, and on the previous evening, when she'd been gathering all the food needed over the holiday, she'd spoken to her mother-in-law.

'Now, Connie's boyfriend is coming on Christmas Day, and I insist that you behave!'

'What ever do you mean?' Madge was outraged.

'You know damned well what I mean. I will not put up with your cantankerous ways, especially then. We don't want any doom and gloom. I want to be able to enjoy Christmas! After all, it's a lot of work for me.' She glared at Madge. 'As you well know, I have to do it all by myself, because you never lift a finger to help.'

'Well, really!'

Dorothy was feeling tired and had no patience left. 'Mess up my Christmas and you'll be sent packing off to Eve's to stay, understand?'

'Perfectly. I think you are being most unkind!'

Dorothy didn't even bother to answer, there was too much to do, but when her husband came home on Christmas Eve she spoke to him about Madge.

'I want you to promise me you'll keep your mother in order on Christmas Day,' she said.

He looked a little surprised at her outburst.

'You needn't look like that, you know what she's like, but Sam will be joining us, and if she misbehaves I'll never forgive her!'

George put an arm around his wife's shoulder and kissed her cheek. 'Relax, love. I know she can be a pain, and I am so grateful to you for putting up with her, but I promised Dad.'

With a sigh she said, 'I know, and you feel it's your duty, but sometimes I could throttle the old devil!'

He started laughing. 'My father often felt the same!'

'What a pity he didn't do so!' Then she turned to her husband. 'I'm sorry, George, I didn't mean that, I'm just so tired and there's a lot to do.'

He gathered her into his arms. 'I know. Now tell me what needs doing.'

'There's the potatoes to peel, the vegetables to prepare, the turkey to be stuffed, mince pies to be made and–'

He stopped her. 'Right, give me the potatoes and veg, a large saucepan and bowl for the peelings ... and a knife.'

She did as she was asked and was very surprised when her husband took them to the table, put them down and spoke to his mother.

'Here, Mum. Peel this lot ready for tomorrow. Dorothy has far too much to do on her own, and we all have to do our bit.'

Madge looked up ready to argue but she saw the expression on her son's face and shut her mouth. Picking up the knife, she started.

George looked across at his wife and winked.

When Connie came home, she made the mince pies, and the family listened to carols being played on the radio whilst George decorated the tree. Dorothy thought she'd never remembered a more delightful Christmas Eve, and after a glass or two of sherry, even Madge appeared in a better frame of mind.

Kay was trying to keep her daughter, Susan, from becoming overexcited about Father Christmas arriving with his gifts. They carefully placed a mince pie, a glass of sherry and some carrots in the fireplace, all ready for the visitor.

'Put them further to the side, Mummy, or Father Christmas will knock the glass over when he comes down the chimney!' Susan demanded.

'How silly of me,' Kay said, hiding a smile. She loved Christmas, but now that Susan was four, the magic of childhood and the festive season was such a joy and something to be cherished. She wondered where John was spending his time and was sad for a moment that this year was no longer one as a family unit. In the past the one thing he did hold sacrosanct was Christmas, when – she had to admit – he took his place as a father with great enthusiasm. But she was determined not to let it spoil the holiday.

At that moment there was a ring on the front doorbell. Kay rose to her feet and opened it. To her great surprise a young woman stood there with an enormous bouquet of flowers.

'Mrs Baker?'

'Yes.'

'These are for you, Madam. Merry Christmas!'

Kay walked into her sitting room and, taking the small envelope from the centre, opened it.

Merry Christmas Kay! Thank you for making my evening so very enjoyable at the Polygon Hotel. I hope to see you again in the near future. Regards, Edward.

She sat down and reread the card then looked at the flowers. There was a mixture of bronze, lemon and red flowers, some seasonal and some not, and she knew they must have cost a small fortune. She couldn't stop smiling. The doorbell rang again.

John stood there, arms full of gifts, looking somewhat uneasy.

'Daddy!' Susan ran to the door.

'You'd better come in,' said Kay.

The next two hours she watched John play with her daughter, thinking how it all could have been so different, had he not been a ladies' man.

He tried to flatter her, but Kay ignored the signals, and then he saw the flowers.

'How beautiful,' he remarked and walked over to them. He picked up the card and read it. 'You haven't wasted any time!' he snapped.

'He's just a business colleague,' she said and felt pleased he was about to leave.

When he'd gone, she picked up the flowers and arranged them in a vase. Well, what a surprise, she thought as she did so. But she was secretly thrilled that the mysterious Edward wanted to see her again. It did a great deal to boost her ego.

Jake Barton sat in his living room, a bottle of whiskey, some ginger ale, a pork pie and a jar of pickled onions on the table. He wasn't bothered about Christmas, it was for families and sentiment, neither of which had any part in his life. Nevertheless, he was feeling pleased with himself. This year had been a mixed one for him, but in the end had turned out very well, thank you very much, he thought as he felt the liquid warm his throat as he drank. Next year promised to be even better – he could hardly wait!

Twelve

Sam arrived at noon on Christmas Day, carrying several gaily wrapped parcels and two bottles of wine. When Connie saw them she looked at him, saying, 'Good Heavens, you look like Santa Claus!'

He kissed her. 'It's Christmas Day after all! Have you all opened your presents yet?'

'No, we usually do that after lunch. They're all round the tree.'

'Then let's put these with them,' he suggested.

He greeted Dorothy warmly, shook George by the hand and smiled at Madge. 'Merry Christmas,' he said.

'Merry Christmas,' she replied, without a smile – and Connie's heart sank.

George poured them both a beer and immediately started talking about the next racing event. Dorothy and Connie grinned at one another, leaving them to chat whilst they carried on with the cooking, the table having been laid in readiness earlier in the morning.

Eventually, it was time to eat. The turkey was succulent, and the meal was eaten with much merriment. Crackers were pulled, mottos read, hats worn and the wine was enjoyed by them all.

Connie noticed that Madge's glass was well topped up by her boyfriend as he chatted to her, trying to get past her frosty demeanour until the alcohol seemed to be doing the trick and she eventually relaxed, to Connie's great relief.

After the meal and the table was cleared, they gathered in front of the tree and the parcels were handed round. Sam had bought a book about touring car racing for George, some perfume for Dorothy and then he handed Madge her gift.

Flushed by the warmth of the fire and the wine she'd drunk, she undid the wrapping with indecent haste and showed an un-expected delight at the beautiful scarf inside.

'It's lovely,' she exclaimed. 'Thank you.'

Connie and her mother looked at each other with raised eyebrows. It was the first time they could remember Madge thanking anyone for anything.

'I thought the colours matched your eyes, Mrs Morgan,' said Sam.

The old girl was rendered speechless.

Sam then handed a small box to Connie. 'I hope you like it, sweetheart.'

Inside was a dainty gold watch.

'Oh, Sam, it's exquisite, thank you.' She leaned forward and kissed him.

He was equally pleased with his gifts too, and so the day went well, with Madge succumbing to the effects of the wine, quietly snoring in the armchair, therefore unable to spoil things for everyone.

At the end of the day, Connie left with Sam. They planned to leave his flat early the next morning, heading for his parents' house in Poole, and apart from making things easier, they wanted to be together as long as possible on their first Christmas.

Snuggled up in bed together Connie chuckled and said, 'You were very crafty with my grandmother, filling her glass so often.'

'I don't know what you mean!' But he too was soon laughing. 'It seemed a good idea. I thought it would loosen her up a bit, that's all.'

'Well, if she becomes an alcoholic, it'll be your fault!'

Letting out a deep sigh he said, 'I really enjoyed today. Thank you for letting me be a part of your family Christmas.'

'Oh, Sam! As long as we were together it didn't matter where we were,' she said, and she kissed him. 'I only hope tomorrow will work out as well.'

He pulled her close. 'My folks will love you, as I do.'

Not everyone had such a good day. John Baker had enjoyed his short visit with his daughter on Christmas Eve and had then spent the rest of the evening among the revellers at a nearby pub. But never had he felt so alone. He missed his family. When he'd walked into the house and seen the tree and all the decorations, smelt the mince pies baking in the oven, he realized just what he'd lost. On Christmas Day he had lunch at a hotel, which made matters worse, as the other tables were filled by families enjoying themselves. As soon as he could, he left and returned to an empty flat. This was no way to live, he decided. Tomorrow, on Boxing Day, he'd ring Kay and see if there was some way they could resolve their differences.

But in the morning, when he tried, there was no reply.

Jake Barton had been to his local pub on Christmas morning. He drank a few beers with Gerry Cooper, followed by a few games of darts, and at two o'clock, when the pub closed for the day, Jake accepted an invitation to have Christmas lunch with him in his somewhat dingy house, cooked by an equally dingy wife, who was mainly ignored by both men as they sat planning for the future.

'We've done really well, so far,' Gerry said, 'but now the building is nearly finished we have to be a bit careful. The next project starts in January and that should be very lucrative.'

'I'm not complaining,' said Jake, grinning,

and he drained the contents of his glass of beer. 'It's all worked out so far. I can't see any problems, can you?'

Gerry shook his head, then put out his hand and touched the edge of the table. 'Touch wood! So far no one has been at all suspicious. We've been too clever for them. What about Edward Harrington?'

'He's as good as gold, no worries there,' Jake assured him.

'Good! Want another beer?'

The drive through the New Forest on Boxing Day morning was enjoyable, and Sam's parents were waiting eagerly to greet them when they eventually arrived in Poole. His mother was a delightful woman, who made Connie more than welcome, as did his father. After lunch, Sam and Connie strolled along the quay, wrapped up against the cold, arms round each other, chatting as they walked.

'There, that wasn't such an ordeal, was it?' he said.

With a look of relief, she answered, 'No, thank heavens. I was a nervous wreck when I arrived, but your parents are lovely.'

'I don't see nearly enough of them,' he confessed, 'but you've seen what it's like when we have to prepare for the next race. There's little time for anything else.' He stopped and took her into a shop doorway, out of the cold.

He enclosed her in his arms and, looking into her eyes, he said, 'If things work out the way I hope in the next few months, I hope that we can put our relationship on a more permanent basis.'

'What are you saying, Sam?' Connie held her breath.

'I'm saying that I want you with me always, sweetheart. I love you, you know that. You're sweet, and I love your innocence. You make me want to protect you from other men. I can't bear the thought of anyone else holding you, making love to you. I want to have been the only man in your life.'

The happiness that had filled her being suddenly plummeted. He must *never* know of her affair with John Baker!

'What's the matter?' he asked.

'Nothing, why?'

'Well, darling, I've just told you I want us to marry in the future, and you frowned. It's not exactly the reaction I was expecting.'

She managed a smile. 'I was just a bit over-come, that's all. I'm thrilled. You must know that I want those things too?' She reached up and kissed him.

'We'll keep our plans to ourselves for a while, that's until the time comes when I feel I'm able, financially, to set up a home for the two of us.'

The festive holiday was soon over and everyone returned to work. Kay was busy typing up reports on the work on various building projects that were near completion and schedules for new work to be started in the New Year. When she'd completed one report, she took it to the chief clerk who scanned through it briefly but with a practised eye.

'This looks fine to me, Mrs Baker. I'm tied up here so would you mind taking it along to the chief architect? His office is on the next floor.'

Kay ran up the stairs and read the plaque on the wall explaining where the various offices were situated, then walked along the corridor until she came to a door with CHIEF ARCHITECT printed on it. She knocked.

'Come in,' a voice called.

She opened the door and saw a figure sitting in front of a large drawing board studying a set of plans.

The man looked up. 'Hello, Kay! This is a pleasant surprise.'

'Edward!' She was robbed of any further words.

He rose from the high stool and walked towards her, took her hand in his and chuckled at her look of consternation.

'Alas, now you've found me out! How are you? Did you have an enjoyable Christmas?'

Recovering her equilibrium, she smiled at him. 'I did, and thank you so much for the flowers, they were lovely.'

'My pleasure. Is that the report I was expecting?'

'Oh, oh yes!' She'd forgotten about it in her surprise. She handed it over and turned to leave.

'Wait!' Edward stepped forward. 'Don't rush off before I've a chance to ask you out to dinner.'

She felt herself blushing.

'Are you free one evening this week?'

'I could be.' She thought quickly. Susan was staying with her grandparents on Friday night. 'How about Friday? It's the only night I have free, I'm afraid.'

'Splendid. Shall I pick you up around seven?'

She felt flustered but tried not to show it. 'That would be lovely, thank you.'

'Until then,' he said, and he opened the door for her.

There was a spring in her step as she returned to her office. So no wonder Edward was treated with such respect. He held an office with great responsibility and power ... and he'd asked her out! Life was looking up. She walked to her desk, humming softly.

Edward walked back to his desk and sat studying the report. He frowned and reread one particular page several times. Surely there was an error here? He picked up the phone and asked to be put through to Kay's office and asked for her by name.

'Mr Harrington on the line for you,' she was told.

Picking up the receiver she answered, 'Kay Baker speaking.'

'Kay, are you sure that the report on the building materials on document three-nine-zero-zero-four is correct?'

She was thrown for a moment; this was not what she was expecting. 'Yes, I am. Was there anything in particular that made you query it?'

'Yes, page four. The list of building materials.'

'I'll double check and let you know,' she said, and hung up. But when she went over her papers, she found no errors at all. Picking up the phone she relayed this to him.

'Thank you, Kay. That's all.'

Edward rang the intercom and asked his secretary to bring a particular file into him, and when she did so, he sat and studied the papers before him. When he finished, he left the office and drove to a building site to talk to the foreman.

The January sales were in full swing, and Tyrell and Greens was full of customers looking for a bargain. Connie and Betty were rushed off their feet most of the day. Once or twice she caught a glimpse of John Baker and thought he looked drawn and grey. She did wonder how he'd spent his Christmas away from his family and, knowing how he idolized his daughter, felt a pang of pity for him. But only for a moment; after all, he'd brought it on himself. She didn't feel so guilty at being a part of his downfall, thinking had it not been her he was seeing, it would have been another woman, and she wondered how his wife was coping. She wouldn't have felt so bad had she known.

It was Friday evening, and Kay was getting ready for her date with Edward, feeling as nervous as a teenager. Going to the office Christmas party alone and meeting Edward by chance was one thing, but tonight was different. It was their first proper date, and she was wondering how she would cope.

She smoothed down the neat black dress she'd decided to wear. Black was safe, and with a string of pearls, with earrings to match, she felt that no matter where they went, she would be suitably dressed. When the doorbell rang, she quickly patted her hair in place and went to open the door.

'Hello,' said Edward, handing her a small bunch of flowers.

'Thank you,' she said, 'how lovely. Come in whilst I get my coat.' Taking him into her sitting room, she left him for a moment.

Looking around the room, he walked over

to a side table and picked up a photograph. There was Kay, a man and a little girl, sitting on a beach beside several rather well-made sandcastles. He looked up as she returned.

'Your daughter and husband?'

'My daughter and soon to be ex-husband,' she said. 'Susan is four, nearly five.' She placed the picture back on the table. 'Ready?'

Edward drove her to the Southampton Yacht Club on the edge of town and walked her to the bar. 'Would you like a sherry, before we eat?' he asked.

They sat in comfortable settees whilst waiting for their table.

'Did you sort the problem of the report I gave you?' she asked, still concerned she may have been at fault in some way.

'Yes, thanks, Kay, it's nothing for you to worry about. Now tell me about Christmas.'

The evening went well. As before, she found Edward easy to talk to. They discussed many subjects, laughed a lot and were at ease with each other.

'You know all about me,' Kay said towards the end of dinner, 'but I know little about you.' Was he married, she wondered and hoped not. She so liked this man but certainly didn't want to get mixed up with someone with a wife. She'd been there.

He laughed heartily. 'Sadly, you have discovered what I do, so no longer can I be a man of mystery, which is such a pity. I rather enjoyed that. In case you're wondering, I'm not married. There was someone once but it didn't work out, which is probably for the best, and since then there hasn't been anyone.'

'I find that very hard to believe. You are a handsome man, sophisticated; don't tell me that there haven't been women who were interested in you?'

He seemed to find this amusing. 'I'm delighted you think these things of me, Kay, my dear, and of course I've enjoyed female company. I'm no monk, you know!' His eyes twinkled with mischief. 'But there is no one of importance in my life – at the moment.' His mouth twitched at the corners as he contained his mirth.

'I do believe you're flirting with me,' she said.

'Oh, but I am, make no mistake about that. Do you mind?'

She grinned broadly. 'No! It's been a long time since that happened to me, and I'm enjoying every moment.'

When he eventually drove her home, Kay invited him in for a coffee, but he declined.

'I won't, thank you, Kay. Not that I don't want to, but a cup of coffee wouldn't be enough – and if you capitulated, I wouldn't know if you did because you're on the rebound. Make no mistake, I want to make love to you, but only because you want *me* as much, not as a substitute for an errant husband.' Before she could reply, he took her into his arms and kissed her.

Thirteen

It was now March, and Sam, with his trusty mechanics, was preparing for another race, this time at Mallory Park Racing Circuit in Leicestershire. As usual, many hours were spent looking over every aspect of the car engine, to produce the fastest time. Eventually, they were satisfied and took it out on the usual trial run at the disused airfield in the New Forest, on the Sunday before the race, which was taking place on the following Saturday.

Connie had gone along to watch, as she would be working on race day and she was anxious to see how things had progressed. There was a chilly wind, and she pulled the collar of her coat up round her neck for added warmth as she stood with Tom, who was holding the stopwatch. Her heart was in her mouth, and she was taut with nerves. Her shoulders ached, her back was stiff and she held her breath as Sam drove to the starting point, knowing how important were the results.

Sensing her anxiety, Tom winked at her. 'Relax, Connie; it'll be fine, you'll see.'

Sam drove over the set course to be timed.

To Connie it looked very fast, but he finally stopped in front of Tom and Harry and got out of the car, saying they needed to adjust something in the carburettor. Then he set off once more.

Even to her unpractised eye, Connie could see this was a faster time ... and it was. Thus satisfied, they loaded the car on the truck and drove to a local pub for a much needed beer and sandwich.

Tucked up behind Sam on his motorcycle on the drive home, Connie held him around the waist and leaned into him as she'd been taught, feeling the warmth of his body, wishing that he didn't have such a dangerous occupation. She'd seen so many pile-ups during the various races she'd attended, and she wondered how long before Sam would be involved in such a scenario. The odds were against him. One day it would happen, and she wondered how she would cope if he was injured. Because of such fears, she was particularly loving when they were in bed that night.

They eventually lay back on the bed, completely exhausted. Sam gazed at her and spoke. 'Well, darling, that was something else! Where did all that come from?'

She couldn't let him know how anxious she was. She stroked his cheek, kissed him softly and said, 'I just wanted to show you how much I love you, that's all.'

'It's just as well I'm going to be away for a few days because a few nights like that and you could kill me off!'

Snuggling into him she murmured, 'You will be careful, won't you?'

'I'm always careful, sweetheart, you know that. I'm not a mad driver like Jake Barton.'

Although Barton was still banned from racing, he kept abreast of the meetings and who was driving and winning, and he knew that Mallory Park was a major race. He also knew that Sam Knight was entering. This stuck in his craw. Although he'd temporarily closed down his garage and was now employed as driver to Edward Harrington and had his own scam on the side, he longed to be part of the racing game again. He'd arranged to have two days off to watch the race and had carefully planned his strategy.

Connie felt somewhat bereft now that Sam had left for the meeting, and because she was unable to be there to see that he came through unscathed, she was very quiet at work. She tried to keep busy but for once she wasn't chattering away to her friend Betty between customers.

'For goodness' sake, Con, do cheer up,' Betty urged. 'You'll chase the customers away with that long face!'

But as much as she tried, Connie felt unable to be her usual cheery self, and she escaped to the stockroom for several items that needed replenishing. As she collected the boxes and turned to leave, John Baker walked in and shut the door firmly behind him. Seeing the predatory expression on his face, Connie became wary.

'I've been watching you this morning,' he said softly. 'You looked so unhappy that I wondered if you'd finished with the boy-friend?' He placed a hand on her arm and squeezed it.

She froze. 'I'm fine, thank you! Now, please, let me pass.'

He stood with his back to the door and re-fused to move. 'I don't like to see you this way, it bothers me. You still mean a great deal to me, Connie darling, I'm sure you know that?'

'Go and find someone else, John. I'm not interested!'

His eyes narrowed. 'How quickly you dismiss me now, when I can remember the time when you couldn't get enough of me! Let me remind you of what you're missing.'

He stepped towards her. Connie's arms were full of boxes, but she was determined to defend herself and quickly brought up her knee and caught him in the groin. He let out a cry of pain and doubled over. She managed to grab the handle of the door and open it. Turning she said, 'You try to touch me again and I'll *really* do you some damage.' As she walked across the floor to her counter, she started smiling for the first time that day.

In the stockroom, Baker's hand was covering his genitals, trying to relieve the pain. Sweat beaded his forehead, and he swore beneath his breath. 'By God, she'll pay for this!'

At Mallory Park, it was race day and the adrenalin was in abundance among the drivers preparing to do twenty laps of the course. Engines revved beneath open bonnets, men in overalls checked the tyres, tanks were filled with petrol and the drivers exchanged their last words with their crews.

Tom had checked the entry list and reported to Sam that the usual drivers were entered and, of course, a few that were new to the circuit. They were always the ones to beware of as they usually lacked the experience of the seasoned drivers.

He patted Sam's shoulder. 'Good luck, mate!'

Sam gave him the thumbs up and drove to the starting line.

It started to drizzle with rain, and Tom frowned. Wet tracks were dangerous.

The noise from the engines was deafening as they waited for the starter to lower his flag. A few minutes later he did so – and

168

then the race began.

Several cars fought for the lead, with one or two very close calls as cars edged too near an opponent, neither giving way until the last moment to avoid an accident that would take them out of the contest. Sam was moving slowly up the field with each lap, but there was a long way to go to the finish line.

It started to rain heavily. One or two of the new drivers came to grief early in the race due to their lack of experience on wet tracks, and the safety crews dashed around removing cars that had come to a standstill, clearing the way before oncoming cars would be endangered. They couldn't move them all, though, so the oncoming traffic had to manoeuvre round them, which was hazardous. A few of the newcomers played it safe, driving carefully, but by so doing were causing a problem for the faster cars, who would soon overtake the stragglers.

Tom cursed beneath his breath. 'Those idiots shouldn't be allowed to enter,' he said as one of the cars veered suddenly, skidding – taking out another vehicle.

Sam was behind the wheel, concentrating on every car that was within his sight, anticipating their next move, his foot on the accelerator, quickly changing gear at every corner before pushing his foot to the floor to drive as fast as was safe. He overtook a straggler safely and then another, but to his surprise the second car suddenly sped up and sat on his tail.

'What the fuck is this man playing at?' he exclaimed as he tried to shake him off. But no matter what he did, the car behind followed, benefiting from the tailwind.

There were six more laps to go, and Sam was now behind the leader, closely followed by his shadow. Sam had to admit whoever was behind the wheel of the other car at his rear was a good driver and he'd have his work cut out to lose him and pass the car leading the race.

On the penultimate lap, Sam saw his opportunity as they approached a corner. He moved to pass the leader on the inside, but the car behind him deliberately drove into the rear of his vehicle, shunting him across the track and on to the grass at the side, narrowly missing the car in front. His car spun three times and ended up crashing into a wall of rubber tyres in front of one of the stands. He was out of the race.

Race stewards ran over to him, fire extinguishers at the ready. He was safely out of the way of oncoming vehicles, but they wanted to check that he wasn't injured and the car wasn't about to burst into flames.

Sam turned off the ignition and climbed gingerly out of the driving seat. He felt bruised and his ribs hurt from the impact. 'I'm all right,' he told the others, 'but who was that bastard who took me out?'

No one seemed to know.

Tom heard the announcement over the loudspeaker. *'Sam Knight is out of the race. His car crashed on the last bend.'* He held his breath. *'But it's all right folks, he's climbing out of the car and walking away. What bad luck!'*

Tom looked at Harry with relief.

Eventually, Sam was reunited with his friends, and he was fuming. 'That bastard took me out deliberately, and I want a word with him!'

'Who was it?' Tom asked.

'I don't know, but I'm bloody well going to find out!' He stormed off.

'There you are,' Tom said to Harry with a broad grin. 'He's fine.'

'Thank God for that! For a moment I wondered.'

Sam found race officials and lodged a complaint. 'Who was the driver of the car?' he demanded.

They looked at the list of entries. 'He's a new driver to us, name of Jim Beckett.'

'Never heard of him. What's he look like? I want a word with him!'

'Don't know, Mr Knight. When I spoke to him he was wearing his helmet.'

'Where did he come in the race then?'

They looked at the result list. 'Way down the list; after all, you overtook him. He was a lap behind.'

Sam was incredulous. 'Of course, but as soon as I passed him, he sat on my tail. He drove well, so what the hell was he doing in that position?'

The official handed the list over to Sam. 'See for yourself.'

After reading it, Sam handed the list back and went searching for the driver, to no avail. He then made his way back to his friends.

'Well, did you find him?' asked Harry.

'No, he's nowhere to be seen. It's all bloody strange if you ask me.'

Tom put a hand on Sam's shoulder. 'Never mind. We live to fight another day. Let's pack up and go home.'

Jake Barton drove back to Southampton feeling well pleased with the outcome of the race. He'd made sure that no one had been able to recognize Jim Beckett, his pseudonym for the day, by wearing his helmet when anyone was near. He'd used another car that he'd worked on in secret so it wouldn't be recognized as belonging to him, and he'd achieved his aim by taking Knight out of the race. It was even more satisfying as Sam had been in prime position to win. Had he not shunted him off the track, Jake knew his nemesis would certainly have been on the winner's podium in first place.

But now Jake would have to keep his head

down and find a place to hide the car he'd used. Besides, he might want to race again. It had felt so good to be back behind the wheel, to feel his heart thumping as he waited to start, the thrill of overtaking – pitting your driving skills against another – but he'd have to steer clear from any race which included Sam Knight for a while. Well, after today, he could live with that.

Fourteen

Kay Baker picked up the mail from the mat as she opened the front door, ready to take Susan to nursery school. She was running late so hurriedly put the two envelopes in her handbag, took hold of her daughter's hand and rushed down the path.

'Come on, darling, Mummy's late,' she urged.

'I'm all right, I'm riding,' chirped Susan and started to gallop, holding the reigns of her pretend horse.

Children's imagination, thought Kay, is a wonderful thing, and this morning it allowed her to arrive at the school gates just in time. She took Susan to the main door, kissed her goodbye and rushed off to catch the bus.

As she sat by the window she relaxed and caught her breath as she saw Edward Harrington's car overtake the bus as it stopped to pick up more passengers. She hadn't seen him since he'd taken her out to dinner, and she had to admit she was disappointed. There was no point in denying it, she was very much attracted to the man, and when he'd told her he wanted to make love to her, but not as a substitute for her husband, she'd been both shocked and excited. Ever since, she'd not been able to get him out of her mind.

He was an object of desire among the typing pool in the office, who thought him sophisticated, dishy, handsome and even more important ... single.

'I wouldn't turn him out of my bed!' said one when he was being discussed during a coffee break.

'Ooh, me neither,' said another.

'I wonder what kind of woman appeals to him?' said a third.

Kay had smiled to herself. *Well, as a matter of fact, ladies, I do!* But he hadn't approached her since.

When she settled at her desk, Kay took out the two letters. One was a bill, but the other was from her solicitors telling her that her divorce would be heard in the local court the following week. It made her feel sad. She still loved John – after all he was the father of her child – but she was no longer *in* love with him, and it brought home to her that their marriage was a failure. It was not something to be proud of.

Between them, their solicitors had come to an agreement over finances. She was to remain in the house. John would pay half the mortgage and give her maintenance for Susan. The savings they had in the bank were to be halved and John could collect any personal articles that were in the house belonging to him. He wasn't contesting the divorce, so she wouldn't see him in court, for which she was grateful. But to this end, she'd had to cite irreconcilable differences as the reason for the divorce, rather than adultery. This way, it would not undermine John's character so much at work. They both knew the divorce would be written up in the local paper and both wanted to play it down as much as possible to save embarrassment all round.

'After all, I have a position to maintain,' he'd said when they met to finally sort things out – and she had agreed. Besides, it was less messy.

Kay hadn't told anyone she worked with about the divorce. All they knew was that she was separated from her husband, and they had no idea who he was at this point and she hoped it would remain so. But the day after the case came to court and the report was in the paper, it was the gossip of the following morning among her colleagues.

'I didn't realize you were married to John Baker at Tyrell's,' said one of the typists. 'Good-looking chap, I always thought.'

'Yes, I thought so too,' said Kay, trying to keep calm.

'Married long, were you?' another joined in.

'Seven years,' said Kay, and as she could see there were many questions yet to be asked she made her excuses. 'Sorry, I've a lot of work on hand,' she said, and she made her escape.

As she walked to her desk, she was called to the telephone. 'Kay Baker speaking.'

'Hello, Kay.'

She recognized the voice immediately. 'Hello, what can I do for you?' She was careful not to give away who was on the line.

'I see you are now a free woman – well, almost – and I wondered if you'd like to come out to dinner with me tonight and celebrate? Or commiserate, whichever is appropriate.'

She had to chuckle at this. 'I would love to!'

'Can you get a babysitter at such short notice?'

'Yes, my mother will look after Susan for me.'

'Splendid. I'll pick you up at seven. See you then.'

She returned to her desk. Yes, it was something to celebrate, she decided. The past was behind her. She'd remember the good days and forget the others. In another six weeks she'd be a free woman – and she wanted to sleep with Edward Harrington!

John Baker realized he was the object of discussion among the staff throughout the store. Whenever he approached any of them, conversation stopped and an embarrassed silence would fall. He did his best to ignore it but was greatly relieved as the end of the working day grew nearer. He prayed it would be a nine-day wonder.

He wasn't the only one to feel this way. Connie had seen the headline in the paper and her heart had nearly stopped beating. STORE MANAGER DIVORCED it said. Taking a deep breath she'd read the report, looking for her name. But it wasn't there. He hadn't been divorced for adultery after all. She shut her eyes and breathed a sigh of relief.

'Thank you, God!' she murmured.

During the following day she'd seen how everyone had reacted towards him and couldn't help wondering what would have happened to her, had she been named as correspondent! It didn't bear thinking about, and Sam, her lovely Sam, had been spared the knowledge of her sordid affair.

When Kay asked her mother to look after Susan and told her she was going out to dinner with Edward, her mother had been pleased.

'Go and celebrate, Kay. It's a new beginning for you. Enjoy it, darling.' She added, 'Susan can stay the night, then you won't need to worry about getting home and putting her to bed.'

Kay knew what she was implying from the way the corners of her mouth were twitching, trying not to smile. 'You are naughty, Mother!'

'Not me, Kay, but with a bit of luck...'She laughed. 'Just be careful, that's all.'

Kay walked down the road shaking her head – her mother! But she thanked God for such an understanding woman. At least if she slept with Edward, she wouldn't feel guilty. But of course he may have very different ideas.

However, when she'd showered that evening, she sprayed her body with cologne and chose her most attractive underwear ... just in case.

Edward was as punctual as usual, looking immaculate in a dark-grey suit, white shirt and striped tie. Kay wondered if there was ever a time when he was dishevelled? Was he a handy man? Did he garden? She realized she knew so little about him ... except that she was attracted to him, liked his company and wondered just how the evening was going to end.

They drove out to the Clump Inn at Chilworth. It was a nice change to get out of the confines of the town. They sat chatting over a drink before choosing from the menu at the bar.

He held up his glass and asked, 'Are we celebrating or drowning your misery?'

'I'm definitely not miserable,' she said,

laughing. 'All right, divorce means failure, but I've decided that I can now start life all over again, without the worry of knowing my husband is with another woman. I have to tell you, that's liberating. So cheers!'

He smiled his approval. 'Cheers, Kay. I'm delighted for you. A liberated woman sounds very promising!'

Over dinner they discussed many subjects, some serious. The situation in Cyprus, how Makarios was an evil influence, how the Queen Mother's horse Devon Loch fell and lost the Grand National – and about the buildings being overseen by the Council.

When they got to the coffee and liqueurs, Edward stared at her and asked, 'Have you still got feelings for your ex-husband, or is that all behind you?'

She hesitated, knowing that her answer was important. 'Because of Susan, there will always be a bond, but apart from that, there's nothing.'

'Are you absolutely sure of this, Kay?'

'Absolutely!'

His expression was unfathomable, and she felt a fluttering of excitement in her stomach as he just gazed at her, as if trying to gauge her conviction. Then he spoke.

'I'm so very happy to hear this, you have no idea.' He looked at his watch, then he asked, 'What time have you to be home?'

Kay felt her cheeks flush as she told him,

'Susan is staying overnight at my mother's. She'll take her to school in the morning.'

'In which case, would you like to come back to my place for a nightcap?'

'Yes, I would.' Her answer was decisive.

He called the waiter over, paid the bill, rose from his seat and, without saying a word, held out his hand.

Kay took it and they walked outside to his car.

Edward didn't speak as he drove and Kay wondered where he lived – was it a house or a flat? She had no idea.

He drove away from Chilworth and then into Basset Avenue, a very prestigious part of the town, and turned into the drive of an impressive-looking house with a manicured front garden that had a small lawn and shrubbery. Kay found herself wondering if he tended the garden himself, or did he employ a gardener?

He stopped the car in front of the large porch, climbed out of the driving seat and came round to her door and opened it. 'Well, here we are.'

The entrance hall was spacious with a large round mahogany table in the centre and a chandelier hanging above it. The staircase was wide with paintings spaced along the cream wall, the stair carpet was a dark, rich green but parquet flooring covered the hallway. It was exquisite.

'Did you design this house, Edward?'

'Yes, I did, do you like it?'

'From what I've seen. It's beautiful, but isn't it too much for one person?'

Chuckling, he said, 'Yes, of course, but when I built it I envisaged it to be a family home, which one day it might be. Come into the sitting room.'

The room was large, light and airy, with French windows leading on to the garden. Two large sofas were either side of the fireplace with a long coffee table in between. A basket of logs sat beside the fireplace, and Kay could envisage sitting there on a cold winter's day, beside a roaring fire, the smell of the logs filling the air. Around the room were other easy chairs, an odd table, here and there, and wall lights and standard lamps lit the room. Although it was all furnished in good taste, it had the warmth of a home – not a showpiece. She was enchanted.

'Oh, Edward, this is beautiful!'

Walking over to one of the tables, he took out a bottle of champagne from an ice bucket, popped the cork and poured two glasses. Handing her one, he said, 'Come and sit down,' and led her to one of the sofas.

As she followed him, she laughed and said, 'You are well prepared.'

He shrugged. 'Well, let's say I was hopeful.' He raised his glass. 'Here's to your liberation!'

They both sipped the champagne.

Putting an arm around her shoulders, Edward asked, 'Have you made any plans for the future?'

'Not really she confessed. 'I'm just glad it's all over. We have sorted the finances. I stay in the house with Susan and, of course, I'll still have to work, but that's as far as it's gone, really.'

'And your ex?'

'He's no longer my concern.'

Staring into her eyes he asked, 'Do you have room for me in your new life?'

'If you want to be part of it, certainly.' She held her breath.

He cupped her chin in his hand. 'I most certainly do,' he murmured and kissed her. Then, taking her by the hand, he led her upstairs.

Kay's heart was pumping wildly as they walked into the bedroom. She'd only ever slept with John and was feeling more than a little nervous.

Sensing this, Edward took her into his arms. 'You don't have to do this, you know ... unless you really want to.'

She put her arms around his neck. 'I do want to, very much,' and this time she kissed him.

They slowly undressed one another, exploring each other's body with tender caresses until they lay on the bed together, entwined. As she ran her hands over his chest, Kay realized how fit he was. His body was muscular, without any spare flesh. The arms that held her were strong, yet he was gentle with her, kissing her eyes, her mouth, her neck, murmuring words of encouragement, helping her to relax as he explored the rest of her body.

Never before had she felt every nerve in her respond to each kiss, each caress, until she was without any inhibition whatsoever. She gave herself to him, completely.

They eventually lay back against the pillows, curled up together, breathless and sated. He kissed her forehead. 'You are a beautiful woman, and that was amazing,' he said softly. He pulled the bedclothes over them, held her close and said, 'Now go to sleep.'

When Kay eventually woke, for a moment she was confused, looking up at a strange overhead light, then she felt an arm close tighter around her. Turning she looked into the blue eyes of her lover. He was smiling.

'Good morning!' He leaned forward and kissed her lightly.

'Hello. What time is it?'

'Seven thirty. You slept well, and so did I. Would you like a cup of tea or coffee?'

'Oh, coffee would be lovely.'

Edward climbed out of bed, walked over

to a chair and put on a dressing gown. He took another from the fitted wardrobe and threw it on the bed.

'Here, put this on. We've got time to have some breakfast and a shower before we leave for the office.'

Kay pushed back the sheet and quickly covered her nakedness with the silk gown.

Edward chuckled. 'You don't have to be shy about your body, Kay. I now know every beautiful inch of it, and I love it!'

She blushed. It was true. She remembered every touch, every kiss.

She followed him downstairs to the kitchen where, to her surprise, Edward made toast, scrambled eggs, bacon and delicious coffee.

'You're very competent in the kitchen,' she remarked as she sat at the breakfast bar.

'I live alone, and I certainly don't intend to starve. Besides, my mother taught me to cook. She said if I was going to university later, she wanted to be sure I could look after myself. I ended up cooking for the other students who shared the accommodation!'

After breakfast they went back to the bedroom. Edward walked into the en suite and turned on the shower. 'Coming?' he asked.

Kay hesitated, and Edward raised his eyebrows.

'There's no need to be shy. If I'm to be part of your life, you'll get used to it. Come on!'

As they stood beneath the large shower

head, Kay thought this was just as sexually exciting as being in bed with this surprising man as he sponged her naked body, before handing the sponge to her. His broad shoulders glistened, his arms enfolded her until she complained and said he wasn't playing fair. He laughed and kissed her longingly. Eventually, he turned off the shower and wrapped her in a large bath towel.

'There! That wasn't so bad, was it?'

She had to admit she'd thoroughly enjoyed the sensation.

As they drove out of the house, Kay said, 'Should we be seen arriving at the office together?'

'Perhaps not. Not until you get your decree absolute. I'll drop you off at the corner, but after that, what does it matter?'

When he stopped the car for her to alight, he kissed her briefly. 'I'm away on business this weekend but I'll call you at home on Monday evening ... and thank you for a wonderful night.'

Kay walked into the office feeling like a new woman. If only her colleagues knew! That would really give them something to talk about. She gave a gleeful chuckle.

Fifteen

Jake Barton arrived at the council garages beneath the Civic Centre and proceeded to wash Edward Harrington's car, in preparation for the morning's rounds of the various building sites to be inspected. It would take up all the morning; outside visits depended on the work in progress. Sometimes it was later than expected. If the weather was bad it could delay the inspection.

At the appointed time, Jake sat waiting. On hearing the familiar footsteps, he alighted from the driving seat to open the door for his employer, who gave him the first address to be visited.

On their arrival, Edward was greeted by the foreman, who handed him a hard hat, and the men walked away, leaving Jake with the car.

He leaned against the vehicle and, taking a cigarette from his pocket, lit it. As he did so, he saw his mate Gerry Cooper walking towards him. Cooper looked furtively around and, seeing no one, wandered over to Jake.

'Any worries?' asked Jake.

'Not as far as I can see,' muttered Gerry, 'so far so good,' and he sloped away.

Meanwhile, Edward Harrington was inspecting some steel girders, piled up on the ground, waiting to be put in place. He frowned. 'These are not what I specified,' he said with some surprise.

The foreman looked concerned. 'But that's what's on the order sheet.'

'Show me,' Edward demanded.

'The sheets are in my office, Mr Harrington.'

'Then let's take a look at them,' said Edward, and the men walked off towards the temporary hut on the site, used as the hub of officialdom during the building of the premises.

Edward studied the sheets in question. 'I don't understand this at all! Here is the strength of girders I ordered, but this is not what was delivered. Those outside will never be strong enough to hold the structure above it!'

'Oh my God, I'd never have noticed. They are due to be placed today.'

'Then stop all work now! Give me the rest of the order sheets; I want to go through them all. Something's not right here, and I want to make sure that's the only mistake before we do anything else.'

Jake was suddenly aware of a change in the atmosphere of the area. Whereas before there had been the usual noise of construction –

188

the banging of hammers, the sound of drilling, the clang of metal – now it was quiet.

He walked over to the corner to see what was going on. The men were standing around talking, smoking, chatting – looking puzzled – but no one was working. He felt a certain tightening in his stomach as he waited.

It was two hours later that Edward Harrington returned to the car. His face was set in grim lines. 'Take me back to the office, Barton,' he said as he stepped into the car.

As Jake drove, he glanced in the mirror at his passenger, who appeared to be deep in thought, poring over sheets of papers. Jake began to feel uneasy.

Sam was waiting outside the staff entrance to Tyrell and Greens at the end of the day, perched on his motorcycle. He thought he'd give Connie a surprise. The staff began to filter out of the building, and he looked up expectantly.

John Baker appeared and saw him sitting there and walked over to him.

'No car today then?'

Sam smiled as he recognized him. 'No, it's being worked on ready for the next race.'

'I suppose all these preparations take up a lot of your time?'

'Yes, pretty much. But there are no short cuts in my business. It's all about safety.'

'Not good for your love life though. Connie likes a lot of attention.'

Sam's eyes narrowed. 'Really? How would you know that?'

John met Sam's puzzled gaze. 'Perhaps you should ask her,' he said and walked away.

Moments later Connie appeared. When she saw Sam she rushed over, flung her arms around him and kissed him. 'I didn't expect to see you here today,' she said, looking delighted.

'No, I thought I'd give you a surprise. Let's go somewhere for a quiet drink, shall we?'

'That's lovely,' she said and climbed on to the back of the bike.

Sam drove to a nearby pub and parked the machine. He seemed a bit subdued.

'Something wrong?' she asked.

'I'm not really sure,' he said, 'but first, what do you want to drink?'

'I'm really thirsty so a shandy would be lovely.' She walked over to a table and watched Sam at the bar. Whatever was the matter, she wondered.

When he came and sat beside her, she asked him. 'What's wrong, Sam?'

He studied her closely as he said, 'I had the strangest conversation with your boss.'

Connie's heart sank. 'Who do you mean? John Baker?'

'Yes. We've chatted before when I was in my racing car waiting for you, and when he saw me tonight, he came over.'

She held her breath. 'Oh, really?'

'He was asking if my work took up much of my time, and when I said it did, he said he didn't think that would suit you. He said you liked a lot of attention. When I asked what he meant, he said I should ask you. What did he mean, Connie?'

She felt sick. The bastard! He couldn't have her, so now he was trying to ruin her life. What on earth could she say?

'I've no idea. Mind you, at the moment I'm his whipping boy! Every week he has it in for someone, and this week it's me. Whatever I did seemed to displease him, so he has been round my department a lot.'

'This isn't the first time you've said he's been giving you grief. If he's upsetting you, sweetheart, I'll have a word with him.'

'For goodness' sake, don't do that! You'll only make it worse; anyway, it'll be somebody else next week.'

Sam didn't look entirely convinced.

'It happens when you work in a big place, Sam. You wouldn't know because you have Tom and Harry who are your mates, but in my world and the world of commerce it's part of life. You just get on with it or get out.'

He stared at her, making her feel uncomfortable. 'Then perhaps you should leave and find a job elsewhere.'

Connie was taken by surprise. She enjoyed her work, and apart from her association with John, there was no reason for her to want to leave.

'But I like my job. I like the store and the people I work with, I'm doing well, why should I leave?'

He shrugged. 'I didn't like the way he spoke. It was as if he was alluding to something else. Something he thought I should know.'

'Like what, for goodness' sake?' she bluffed.

'That's what I'm asking you, Connie.'

She tried to control the fear building inside her. If Sam thought for a moment there was something between her and her manager, she knew she'd lose him.

'Oh, for God's sake!' She pretended to be outraged. 'Don't you trust me? This is beginning to feel like a third degree. You're cross-questioning me here as if I'm on trial, and I don't like it, and if you don't stop this minute, I'm walking out of here!'

At last he was convinced. 'I'm sorry, darling, I didn't mean to upset you, I just didn't like his attitude, that's all.'

'You should work for him, then you'd understand the man. Now can we have a decent conversation?'

To her great relief he dropped the matter, and when he took her home he kissed her lovingly before taking his leave.

Connie went straight to her bedroom and flung herself on to the bed. She felt drained.

'Bloody hell, that was close,' she muttered. She was going to have to do something about Mr Baker. She couldn't let him get away with this or goodness knows what he'd say next.

The man in question was standing on the doorstep of his old home, ringing the bell, feeling like a stranger. He'd arranged to take away his belongings, which Kay had packed for him, and he resented having to wait to be let into what he still considered to be his home. Yes, he'd rented a one bedroom flat, but in his bones he thought of it as a temporary arrangement.

Kay opened the door. 'Hello, John. You'd better come in.'

As he shut the door behind him, she pointed to two suitcases on the floor in the hallway. 'Well, here you are. I think I've put in everything that's yours. If I've missed something, then let me know once you've unpacked.'

Kay just stood waiting.

'Don't I get offered a cup of coffee? I could kill for one, as I've come straight from work. Surely that isn't asking too much, is it?'

She hesitated for a moment. 'Oh, very well.'

He followed her to the kitchen, taking in all the details around him which were so familiar. He was surprised how much it hurt.

'Where's Susan? I was hoping to see her.'

'Mother's taken her to Brownies. She joined a few weeks ago.' She put the kettle on. 'So how are you, John? Keeping well?'

He sat on a chair. 'How very cold you sound, Kay. You wouldn't think we'd been married and had a child.'

'But now we're not!'

'And that's it, is it? Don't you have any regrets at all?'

She made the coffee and handed it to him. 'Regrets, me? How strange you think that I'm the one who should feel sorry when it was your womanizing that caused our divorce in the first place!'

'You don't pull your punches, do you? All right, I admit it was my fault, but we could have worked it out.'

'Don't be ridiculous! You will never change.' She leaned against the kitchen sink. 'Now I no longer have to wonder who you're with because it doesn't matter any more.'

'You've changed, Kay. You're so different.'

'Well, John, one of us had to ... and yes, I am a different woman. I am in charge of mine and Susan's lives now, and if I'm honest, they're much better than before, so I suppose you did us a favour!'

He gazed at her, not knowing what to say for a moment. 'You're not legally free for another six weeks.'

She just laughed scornfully. 'I can wait.'

'And what then? Will you start dating

194

other men?'

'That is none of your business! Now if you don't mind I need to get on.'

He had no choice but to collect his belongings and leave. After he'd put the suitcases into the boot of the car, he climbed into the driver's seat, started the engine and just as he put the car into gear, another car pulled up. A tall, well-dressed man climbed out and walked up to the front door.

John waited to see what happened and was more than a little surprised to see Kay let the man inside. Who the hell was he? He drove away, still wondering.

Kay had been surprised to open the door to Edward Harrington. She'd thought it was her ex-husband who'd perhaps forgotten something.

'Edward! Come in.'

'I hope you don't mind me dropping in unannounced,' he said, 'but I've had a hell of a day and just felt the need to see you.' He pulled her close and kissed her.

Kay felt all the tension from her previous meeting melt away as she returned his kisses. Letting out a deep sigh she said, 'Of course not. I'm always happy to see you. Would you like some coffee?'

'That would be lovely. Where's your little girl?'

'Mother's taken her to Brownies.'

'So we're alone?'

She nodded. 'Completely.' She saw the intensity of his gaze. 'Never mind the coffee,' she said and held out her hand. They walked up the stairs together.

Sixteen

John Baker drove away, silently seething. There was no man in Kay's life, she said – she had lied! So that's how she could be so cold towards him. It hadn't taken her long to find a replacement!

In his present mood he failed to see the irony of the situation. It had always been he who had someone on the side, but now it was his ex-wife who was stepping out and he didn't like it one bit! He drove back into town and pulled up outside a nearby pub. He needed a drink.

Sam and his two mechanics had had a long day and they were tired. As they locked up the garage Sam said, 'Come on, you two, let's go to the pub and have some food and a pint. My treat.'

The Spa Tavern was one the boys used frequently. It was unprepossessing but served good bar food. They walked in and ordered a pint of beer each and chicken and chips for three. Taking their beer with them the three men found an empty table and sat down with a sigh of relief, knowing their day was over and they could relax over a decent meal.

Sam took out a packet of cigarettes and lit one. At the same time he gave a cursory glance around the room and was surprised to see Connie's boss sitting at the bar, alone. He hoped the man wouldn't see him because the last thing he wanted now was a conversation about car racing. He just wanted a drink with his mates and some food.

They were halfway through their meal when John Baker saw Sam as he downed the dregs of his drink, got off his stool and walked to the gents. The sight of the driver infuriated him, and he'd had enough alcohol to highlight his mood. As he stood at the urinal, his temper didn't improve. He was filled with spite. Spite about his wife entertaining a man in *his* house and, who knows, maybe *his* bed, and then spite against the man who was taking his place with young Connie, who had, like his wife, turned her back on his advances. He washed his hands and left the gents. He hesitated for a moment only, then he walked towards Sam's table.

Sam saw him coming but continued to talk to Tom in the hopes that the man would walk past without speaking. It was not to be.

'Good evening, Mr Knight. I'm surprised to see you here.'

Sam smiled. 'Hello. Just taking much needed sustenance after a heavy day. You know how it is.' He noticed the slight slur-

198

ring of Baker's speech, realizing he'd been in the bar for some time.

'Not seeing young Connie tonight then?'

There was something in the other man's tone that made Sam wary. 'No, not tonight.'

'Never mind, she'll be worth waiting for.' His mouth tightened into a narrow mean line. 'You may be a winner on the racetrack, but as far as Connie's concerned, I got there in first place!'

Sam got to his feet in a flash, eyes blazing with anger. 'How dare you talk about my girl like that!'

He moved towards Baker, but Harry caught hold of his arm and pulled him back in his chair as Tom got to his feet, took John Baker firmly by the arm and manhandled him out of the pub. Once outside he spoke. 'You had no right to say that,' he said. 'It was very unwise of you.'

John, now pleased with himself, grinned broadly. 'Oh, I have every right. She's not the little innocent your mate thinks she is.'

'Now you just shut your mouth before I do it for you!' Tom stood over him menacingly, and Baker shook off his hold.

As he staggered away, he called back over his shoulder, 'Sam Knight needed to know, that's all – and now he does.'

Tom watched him to make sure he wasn't going to make more trouble and, taking a deep breath, returned to the bar.

'What else did he have to say?' Sam demanded.

'Nothing. The man was drunk. Take no notice.' He sat down, glancing briefly at Harry, who just raised his eyebrows.

Pushing his unfinished meal away, Sam got to his feet. 'I'll see you two in the morning.'

When they were alone, Tom told Harry what Baker had said to him outside.

'Bloody hell!' exclaimed Harry. 'He's put the cat among the bleeding pigeons and that's a fact.

'Well, it's none of our business. It's for Sam and Connie to sort out.' He grimaced. 'I do hope it doesn't spoil things for those two; they're so right together.'

'How would you feel if you were in Sam's place right now?' asked Harry.

'Not good.'

'Exactly!'

Sam walked to the park and sat on a wooden bench, stunned by what he'd heard. What made it even worse was that he believed Baker. The old saying 'a drunken man speaks a sober mind' kept racing through his head. It wasn't the first indication Connie's boss had made that something was amiss. He remembered an earlier conversation where he'd said Connie needed a lot of attention and had told Sam to ask her what he meant. He remembered her excuse. She had lied to him! What a fool he'd been to protect her innocence ... as he thought.

He remembered when they had first made love. He'd been puzzled that there had been no show of such innocence, but sometimes with young girls this was so and he'd dismissed it. Why wouldn't he?

He closed his eyes in an effort to shut out his disappointment. But all he could think of was Connie in Baker's arms – making love. It was not a pretty thought. What was he going to do about it? How could he feel the same about her now? He slowly shook his head. His thoughts were driving him crazy. He rose from the bench and walked home.

Kay Baker lay back entwined in Edward's arms, beneath the sheets. The heat from his naked body against hers. She didn't know when she had felt so happy. She gazed into the blue eyes that were looking at her and ran a finger across his mouth.

'Mmm,' she murmured, 'that was so good.'

He chuckled softly. 'I'm so happy to know that I please you.'

She rolled on top of him and slowly kissed him. 'I'm happy to put it in writing if you like.'

'Well, Kay darling, a good reference never goes amiss.'

Laughing she said, 'Would you like that cup of coffee now? Only, Susan will soon be home from Brownies.'

He held her even tighter. 'That's such a shame as I'm so very comfortable, but it wouldn't do for your mother to find us in bed together.'

She rolled off him. 'You don't know my mother!'

They were sitting at the breakfast table in the kitchen when Susan rushed in followed by her grandmother, waving a new badge in her hand.

'Look, Mummy, I got a badge for my knots tonight!' She stopped when she saw Edward. 'Hello! Would you like to see my badge?'

'I certainly would,' he said. And proceeded to inspect it carefully.

Kay introduced him to her mother.

He shook hands with her and then said, 'Thank you for the coffee, Kay. I'll be in touch.' He leaned forward and kissed her on the cheek, then said goodbye to the child and Kay's mother.

'I'll call you,' he said as Kay let him out of the front door.

When she returned to the kitchen, her mother smiled at her. 'What a lovely man! I do hope we didn't come home too early?'

Kay felt her cheeks flush.

'I see we didn't, I am so pleased for you. Come along, Susan, let's get you undressed and in the bath whilst Mummy gets us something to eat.'

Connie climbed out of bed on Sunday morning and stretched. She hadn't heard from Sam at all during the week which was unusual. She assumed he was too busy – after all, he'd warned her of such times. She'd walk to the garage this morning and see if he was there.

When she arrived outside, she couldn't hear any noise at all. The radio, which was usually blaring out, was silent, there was no banging or sounds of work in progress, but Sam's motorbike was parked outside and one door was slightly ajar. She entered.

'There you are!' she exclaimed.

Sam was sitting on an upturned box, staring into space. He just looked at her, without speaking.

'Are you all right, darling?' she asked.

'No, I'm not, since you ask.'

The coldness in his voice surprised her. He'd never ever spoken to her like that. Usually, his tone was warm and loving. It was as if there was a solid wall of ice between them, and she didn't know what to do. She didn't feel able to put her arms around him, as was her habit.

'Whatever is wrong?' she asked with some trepidation.

He looked straight at her, his jaw set. 'You lied to me, Connie!'

She felt her stomach plummet.

'You led me to believe you were an innocent young girl, and I believed you, but you lied. How could you do that to me?'

'What do you mean?'

'I was not the first man to make love to you after all. John Baker had you first!'

She felt the bile rise in her throat. Oh my God, he knew! She closed her eyes for a second, her mind racing to find the right words – and failing miserably. She tried to fight the tears which began to fill her eyes. She blinked rapidly.

'I'm sorry, Sam, really I am. I didn't tell you in case I lost you.'

His gaze didn't waver. 'He's not only so much older than you, but he's married, for God's sake! Didn't you ever consider his wife?'

There was no further point in lying, she thought. Better to get things out into the open. After all, what choice had she? 'To be honest, no, I didn't. I was nineteen, young, impressionable. He was smooth, sophisticated. I was flattered by the attention ... and one thing led to another. But I ended it with him as soon as we met. I love you, Sam. Please believe me!' She brushed a tear from her cheek. 'Please don't let this spoil things for us.'

There was such an expression of sadness in his eyes; she thought she'd break down altogether. 'Nothing can ever be the same, Connie, don't you see? I loved you, trusted you. I cared about you being a young innocent young woman. I loved that about you and the fact you trusted me to take care of you, when all the time...' He couldn't carry on.

'Don't you still love me?' she asked, her voice barely above a whisper.

'I don't know how I feel about you at the moment, and that's the truth.'

'Oh, Sam,' was all she could say.

'You'd better go home, Connie.'

'But I can't leave things like this!' she cried, gesticulating madly with her hands as if imploring him to say something positive.

'I'm sorry, but I've got to have time to think. Go home, please.'

She had no choice and walked slowly to the door, where she paused. 'I do love you, Sam, with all my heart, and I pray you can forgive me for deceiving you. I've grown up since I met you and I now know what's important in my life – and that's you, Sam. Nothing or no one else!'

She walked down the street, her shoulders hunched in rejection, the tears now flowing, unhindered. Her life in ruins.

Seventeen

Gerry Cooper was in a major panic. All work on the building site had ceased ever since Edward Harrington had called to inspect the work in hand, and Gerry thought his scam was about to be discovered. He'd been given the job of ordering the materials for the building. All he'd had to do was take the order form to the suppliers and hand it over, but he'd hatched upon a scheme with one of the workers there. They'd ordered the supplies, but using inferior cement and girders that were lighter and cheaper, pocketing the difference between them and Jake Barton. Jake had acted as a lookout for any trouble from Harrington in case he'd discovered their plan and earned a cut of the profits for so doing. Until yesterday, things had run smoothly. Now the scheme had been discovered and Gerry was trying to find a way that wouldn't implicate him.

He had no choice but to warn his associate at the suppliers, who had immediately given in his notice and left Southampton without telling Gerry.

Edward, when he suspected the reason for the discrepancies, had called in the police and had instructed the workforce to go over the building, testing everything that had been used on parts of the building that had already been constructed.

The results were catastrophic!

A meeting had been called at the Civic Centre, where everyone at the top of the committee dealing with all the building, past and present, had been called. It was only then that Edward was able to give them the bad news.

'The unfinished building is unsafe, gentlemen. We will have to dismantle everything and start again!'

There was pandemonium around the table. Cries of, 'That will cost thousands!'

Another said, 'We don't have the budget to rebuild!'

And so it went on.

Many tried to apportion the blame. 'Who is responsible for this? Surely someone is at fault for letting such a thing happen?'

All eyes looked at Edward.

'Gentlemen, whoever planned this did it with great precision. My foreman had no reason to doubt that the building materials delivered were not the ones that had been ordered. After all, he followed my instructions to the letter. The invoices were clearly marked to supply the goods we had talked about whilst going over the plans. As far as we were concerned, there was nothing amiss.

I have called in the police to look into it. Whatever happened, it was when the invoices left our hands. When everything was delivered it was checked against the invoices and the number of items tallied. What we didn't know was that the actual supplies had been tampered with.'

There was more huffing and puffing from those around the table as Edward said, 'Unfortunately, the council will have to cover the cost of dismantling the building as we cannot leave it standing as it is.'

The committee had no recourse here and had to agree, but it was a very frosty atmosphere in the room as they left after the meeting.

Edward let out a deep sigh and walked to his office. Standing by the window, looking out at the cars, and at the pedestrians going about their daily lives, he was dispirited. He took great pride in his work, and if anything was wrong, it reflected on his professionalism. He'd been proud of this rebuild. It was for a block of offices built on two floors to be used by the council. Much-needed space for the staff. It had been simplistic in design but with his usual flair – and now it would have to be destroyed! Who could have done such a thing? Had this remained undiscovered, at some time in the future the building would have collapsed, perhaps causing fatalities. Well, the police were now making their enquiries, and he prayed they'd find the perpetrators of such scandalous behaviour!

He sat at his desk. The one good thing in his life at the moment was Kay. Thank God for her! At least when he was with her, he could put all these worries out of his mind for a short while. He smiled softly as he thought of little Susan and her badge for tying knots. Could he envisage taking on another man's child? He had to contemplate such a move if his relationship with Kay was to grow and mature.

He was falling in love with her, of that there was no doubt. Already he could see her living in his house, cooking in his kitchen, curled up with him on the settee before a log fire. Sharing his bed. He wanted her in his life on a permanent basis, but he would have to wait. After all, her divorce was so recent. She deserved a bit of freedom, time to make up her mind about once again taking on the trappings of marriage. Well, there was no rush; he'd been single for a long time, and another few months wouldn't matter. In any case, he had to get this present situation sorted first, before making any personal plans of his own.

Jake Barton and Gerry Cooper were in Jake's kitchen poring over their predicament.

'That bastard at the suppliers has upped

sticks and pissed off out of it!' Gerry declared angrily. 'I was good enough to give him the nod about the situation and the next thing he'd buggered off!'

'How do you know that?'

'I rang the place to talk to him this morning and they told me. I went round to his gaff and it was empty.'

'Where does that leave you then?'

'Holding the fucking baby if they find out, that's where!'

Jake frowned. 'So what's the next move?'

'I'm keeping a low profile at the moment at work. I'm hanging on there for the time being as then if anything's happening I'll know about it. If I have to, I'll scarper.'

'Can they find anything to put you in the frame for this?'

Gerry looked uncertain. 'Nothing they could prove now my mate has scarpered. I would just deny all knowledge and throw the ball into his court. After all, I just handed over the order form and took delivery. I'm no builder; I'm just the gofer, so how would I know if anything was wrong?'

'But if they go looking for your pal and find him and he drops you in it, what then?'

'If they find the rotten bugger, you won't see me for dust! I'll be off to the smoke; they'll never find me there.'

Jake wasn't convinced. 'Well, let me tell you, Gerry, if you try to implicate me, you won't have enough breath in your body to make the journey! Do I make myself clear?'

The other man nodded. Although he and Jake were cohorts in this scheme, he knew enough about him to know he had a dangerous side, one not to invite.

'It'll be fine, you'll see.' But he was a worried man.

Connie too was worried but for different reasons of course. Sam had not contacted her, and as the days passed, she grew severely depressed.

The day after Sam had told her he knew about her affair, she tackled John Baker. She'd seen him across the floor and marched over to him. 'I want to talk to you!' she demanded.

He looked round furtively in case anyone had heard her raised voice and walked her to the stock cupboard, closing the door behind them.

Connie lifted her hand and smacked him hard around the face. He was astonished! His cheek stung, and he put his hand to his face.

'You bastard! You couldn't let go without being vindictive and trying to ruin my life. I'm sure it gave you great pleasure!'

Seeing the anger seething in her eyes, he suddenly realized he was on dodgy ground as Connie had threatened to go to his boss and accuse him of sexual harassment.

'I'm really sorry, Connie. I got drunk and your boyfriend came into the bar. I just lost it. I do apologize. I didn't mean to make trouble for you.'

Her rage didn't diminish. 'You're a bloody liar, John! They just trip off your tongue like water, but then I must remember you've had a lifetime of practice.'

'You're not going to do anything foolish, are you?'

She calmed down and glared at him. 'Believe me I aim to get my own back, but in my own time. So every day you'll wonder if this is the day the managing director calls you into his office. Because I swear to you – one day he certainly will!'

Baker looked at the closed door which had been loudly slammed as Connie made her exit. He was shaken. He had no doubt that she meant every word, but there was nothing he could do to stop her. His only hope was that eventually she might change her mind as each day passed, but if she lost her man through him, he knew he was in deep trouble.

On her way home, Connie stopped at a phone box and, putting her pennies in the slot, dialled the number of the garage. 'Knights Repair Shop.'

Connie recognized Tom's voice. 'Hello,

Tom, could I speak to Sam, please?'

'Hello, Connie love.' He glanced over at Sam, who vigorously shook his head. 'Just a minute, Connie, I'll get him,' he said, and he put down the receiver.

Walking over to Sam he said, 'You have to talk to the poor girl, you can't just ignore her, it isn't fair!'

Reluctantly, Sam walked across the garage floor and picked up the receiver. 'Hello, Connie.'

Hearing his voice brought a lump in her throat. She had missed him so much. 'Hello, Sam. I can't go on like this much longer. Every day is a nightmare wondering if I'll ever see you again. I love you so much, darling. Please don't do this to me.'

He could hear the anguish in her voice, and it tore at him. He did love Connie, but he was still hurting from what he saw as her betrayal. Even so, he did miss her and now, listening to her, he didn't know what to say.

'Can't we meet and talk about this and see if we can't find a way out? Please, Sam, don't say no. If you do meet me, I won't ask anything else of you, ever again. I promise. If you decide after it's over between us, I'll keep out of your life.'

How could he say no? 'I'll meet you out-side Timothy Whites the chemist at seven thirty tonight, then we'll talk.'

He heard her sigh of relief. 'I'll be there,

Sam,' she said.

As he walked back to the car, Tom took him by the arm. 'That girl worships the ground you walk on; don't let your pride get in the way tonight when you meet. She's a little diamond.'

Sam didn't reply.

Connie arrived early. To relieve the tension which stiffened every bone in her body, she studied the contents of the display in the window, stamped her feet against the cold. Walked up and down, wondering what this meeting would achieve. She dreaded being told that Sam no longer wanted to be with her. If only he would give her a second chance, she would never let him down, ever. He was her life, and she couldn't bear the thought of being without him.

'Hello, Connie!'

Sam had walked up behind her. She turned and looked into his eyes, trying to gauge his expression, but failed.

'Hello, Sam, it's lovely to see you, thank you for coming.'

His heart went out to her as he heard the uncertainty in her voice, saw the sadness in her eyes and he wanted to reach out and hold her, but he didn't.

'Come on, it's bloody freezing out here; let's find a quiet corner in a pub where we can talk.'

She walked beside him, not touching him. Not walking too close. Feeling like a stranger beside him.

They soon found a bar and a table. Sam bought the drinks and sat down.

Connie waited for him to speak.

'You look tired,' he said.

'It's been a busy day.' She studied the face that was so dear to her. 'How are you, Sam?'

'Miserable, Connie, if I'm truthful. Yes, that just about sums me up at the moment.'

She went to reach across the table to take his hand, then changed her mind. 'I'm sorry you feel like that, but I am just the same. Oh, Sam darling, I miss you so much and I could tear my heart out for being the cause of your unhappiness. If I could turn the clock back I would.'

'But you can't, Connie, sadly.'

'No, I can't. What can I say but I'm sorry? I was stupid, I was flattered and it went to my head.' She stared into his eyes. 'Have you never ever made a mistake and wished you could turn clock the back too?'

He had to smile. He was an honest man if nothing else and he recalled many a misdemeanour in his youth which he had regretted later.

'Oh yes, Connie. I'm not perfect you know. We all make mistakes and should learn from them, but it's the fallout we have to cope with sometimes and that can be painful for all concerned.'

'Can you truthfully tell me you no longer love me, Sam?' She held her breath. If he said no, all was lost.

As he looked at her, Connie anxiously awaiting his answer, in his mind he heard Tom's voice: *'Don't let your pride get in the way.'* He reached across the table and took her hand. 'No, Connie. I can't say that.'

She felt the tears of relief brim her eyes. 'Oh, Sam,' was all she could say.

'But no more lies, Connie. Not ever!'

She was too overcome to speak but just shook her head rapidly.

Seeing that she was about to burst into tears he said, 'Come on, drink up. We'll buy some fish and chips and take them home.'

She happily did as she was told, and this time he held her hand as they walked out into the cold.

As they sat in Sam's flat eating, the conversation was stilted. They talked around safe subjects. His hopes for the next race, the car he would drive. The atmosphere was strained, and Connie was on edge the whole time. When it was time to leave, she was relieved. She realized that she would have to be patient, tread carefully and keep her fingers crossed that in time things would get better.

Eighteen

As the weeks passed, the police were no nearer to solving Edward Harrington's problem regarding the exchange of building materials. They had discovered the man at the suppliers who had dealt with the invoices was missing and as yet had been unable to trace him. It was stalemate. The half-built building in question had been demolished and the site cleared once again, at great expense – and the rebuild put on hold. Gerry Cooper and Jake Barton went about their business somewhat nervously but in the clear ... for the time being.

Jake had planned to give up his post as Harrington's driver in a month's time, which was when his six-month ban from racing had passed. He couldn't wait to get back on the circuit and regain his position. He'd hired two new mechanics to help him prepare his car, which had been laid up in the garage, under wraps during his fallow months. Besides, he wanted to distance himself from the architect as soon as possible, and to this end he handed in his notice.

Edward wasn't surprised. He knew Jake's history on the racetrack and had long realized that was the only thing of importance in the man's life. He wasn't sorry. Jake had served him well as a driver but he wasn't a likeable man. He had no conversation or personality. Edward had it in his mind to do his own driving in the future, to cut down the cost. He felt duty bound to try after the debacle of the build and the added expenditure.

Sam and Connie were slowly rebuilding their relationship. She had the sense to realize she had to take things slowly. Sam was still a little distant at times, which cut her to the quick, but she knew she had to continue to be patient to win back his trust. This was helped by the imminence of the first touring car race of the year. The preparations were in hand, and Connie spent her Sundays at the garage, making tea and trying to be useful. Here, she found a staunch ally in Tom.

'Just give him time, love,' he told her as they washed up the cups after a lunch break. 'Sam was devastated, you know that. But he loves you, Connie. He'll get over it.'

And so it seemed. As the days passed and the race drew nearer, Sam was more relaxed with her, and when she lay in his arms at night, he seemed to lose the slight coolness that had remained for some time – until, after one particular night of passion, it seemed to disappear altogether. Now she really believed they had a chance. Until that point she'd never been sure.

Connie had decided against causing trouble for John Baker. What was the point? She and Sam were together again, which was the more important thing in her life. Revenge against John was pointless, and it would open up a can of worms she could well do without ... and to what end? Apart from which, she'd recently been promoted. She was now in charge of the haberdashery department. The person who'd previously been in charge of the purchasing had retired, and Connie had been asked to take their place after she'd suggested new products to be tried, which had been successful. The management had been impressed with her ideas, and they had borne fruit. Any scandal would certainly have put this new position in jeopardy, so a still tongue was the best answer. She was thrilled with her promotion at such a young age, and Sam was delighted for her.

'Well done, sweetheart. I always knew you were a bright girl!'

His compliments warmed her heart. John Baker had not been near her to congratulate her, for which she was thankful, but he had realized that now he was probably safe from being exposed by his past lover and had moved on to another new young assistant.

At least he was now a free man to do so, thought Connie, who just watched with amusement as he went out of his way to charm his new acquisition. She wondered how long it would take him to get the girl into bed. Well, she mused, at least she'd have a good time, because he was a good lover.

The repairs and tweaks to Sam's car were nearly complete, and he and his two mechanics were pleased with the speed they had managed to achieve. But new drivers were coming along now, and there was no way of knowing how good the competition was. He was also aware that Jake Barton would again be racing against him. All he could do was be prepared and drive well. He couldn't wait to be back on the track, because it was what he enjoyed doing the most. It was his life, and as the day grew nearer, he felt the adrenalin begin to flow through his veins.

The meeting was to be held at Brands Hatch on a Sunday, following time trials to sort the starting position of the drivers on Saturday.

Connie travelled to the track on Sunday by train as Sam had a meeting earlier in the day. Sam was to talk to a man about a car he wanted Sam to work on for a different race class, and of course this would be an important step in Sam's future plans.

Connie was greeted warmly by Tom and

Harry when she did arrive. She enjoyed the banter from the two men of whom she'd grown so fond. The bond between the three men was something special, she always thought. They were really a great team, and apart from being the backbone of Sam's success, they would also be a major part of the workforce as his dream of building engines for racing cars became a reality.

Connie felt the tightening of every nerve in her body as they started to prepare for the race. Sam had kissed her briefly when she arrived, but then got down to business on the car. This was her cue to stand back. She wandered around the other areas, looking to see if she recognized any of the other drivers from previous meetings. In the distance she saw Jake Barton with two men, tuning the engine of his Jaguar. Her heart seemed to miss a beat when she recognized him. There was something evil about this man, she felt, and it worried her when he was in a race with Sam. She prayed that today he would not cause any problems – and walked back to her own team.

Jake Barton was in his element on the racetrack and could hardly wait to begin, but he had the sense to know he'd have to be careful. The authorities would be watching him like a hawk after his ban, just waiting for him to make a mistake, and then he'd be out of the race-game for good. Well, no way was that going to happen. He'd toe the line ... for a while, anyway. He'd seen Sam arrive and his crew. The same old feelings of jealousy arose – that would never go away. He still felt he was the better driver, but he knew that for once he had to think sensibly to be able to continue, so he shut his mind to his rival. Today he'd be a model driver, but he'd still push to be as near to the front as possible.

The race was about to begin, and the cars were in their positions, engines revving, nerves taut, then the flag went down and the cars took off, heading for the first bend. Connie held her breath as several vehicles moved in a block and she wondered who was going to collide, but they all rounded the bend safely.

Connie's body was stiff with tension, and she tried to relax her aching shoulders as she watched the cars pass her vantage point time and time again. Sam was moving up the field steadily with each circuit, closely followed by two new drivers and Jake Barton. The new drivers showed their skill as they weaved in and out, overtaking other vehicles who were either slower or had been shunted out in collisions. But as she stood watching the cars approaching in the distance, Connie held her breath. Three cars were in a line, moving at speed. There was Sam, a new driver and

Jake Barton. Someone was going to have to give way to prevent a collision, but as they drew nearer, it seemed that no one was going to do so. She grabbed hold of Tom's arm and held on, scarcely breathing.

They stood rooted to the spot as they watched the cars get nearer and nearer. Connie closed her eyes, unable to watch, quietly praying. 'Please don't let Sam crash!'

She heard the sound of an engine change and opened her eyes to see Sam suddenly forge ahead of the other two, leaving them to make the corner as best they could. All three made it safely, but it was a very close thing. Barton's wing scraped the other car as they both rounded the bend, but the other driver managed to keep control of his vehicle, and they soon were out of sight.

Connie let go of Tom's arm. 'Bloody hell!' she muttered. 'I'll be a basket case before this race is over.'

He rubbed his arm. 'Do me a favour, girl; hang on to something else next time, will you?'

She immediately apologized.

'Here,' he said, handing her a cigarette, 'I think we both need one of these.'

The race wasn't without incident, and several cars came to grief. One driver was taken away by ambulance and some cars were badly damaged, but Sam came second, with Jake Barton in third place.

As they stood on the rostrum, Sam turned to Jake and held out his hand. 'Congratulations,' he said. 'That was a great race.'

Jake looked at the outstretched hand and then looked at Sam with an insolent grin. 'You were lucky this time, Knight. But next time I'll beat you, see if I don't!' He then walked away.

Sam just shook his head. Well, at least he'd tried, he thought, but it was a complete waste of time trying to appeal to Jake's good nature – because the man didn't have one!

That evening, the four of them went out to dinner to celebrate, before driving home. Sam was tired but elated. He'd done well in the race, and he now had a contract to build an engine for another racing driver in a higher class. His first commission – and he was thrilled.

'This is the start I needed, Connie love. Once this engine has been built, and raced, it will prove my skills and should be the start of a lucrative business. Word of mouth is the best recommendation, and this chap had been told about me by another driver, whose engine I'd tuned.' He kissed her. 'We're on our way, sweetheart!'

Connie was thrilled for him and related the happy news to her father when she returned home.

He too was delighted. 'The boy seems to

be doing really well, love. I'm happy for him. When I talked to him at that race meeting I thought he had his head screwed on ... and I liked him.'

Madge, who had been eavesdropping, chimed in. 'Perhaps then he'll make an honest woman of you!' she said in her usual blunt fashion. 'I don't agree with you staying at his place when you're not even engaged. It's not decent!'

'What I do, Nan, is none of your business, and I can do without your snide remarks, thank you!'

As Madge opened her mouth to argue, George intervened. 'If Dorothy and I as Connie's parents have no objections, then your remarks are out of place and unwelcome, Mother.'

The old girl huffed and puffed but said nothing further. But her look of disgust at the whole thing was enough to show her feelings.

Connie kissed her mother and father goodnight, ignored her grandmother and went to bed. But the remarks niggled at her. She wanted to marry Sam Knight more than anything, and she wondered just how long she'd have to wait until he did propose to her. She hoped it would be sooner rather than later; she couldn't wait to move away from such a bitter old woman who seemed to make it her life's ambition to be disagreeable.

On Monday morning at the store there was to be a meeting with heads of department in the managing director's office. It was Connie's first since becoming head of haberdashery, and she was nervous. Collecting the necessary papers, she made her way to the lift. She and John Baker arrived together. Ignoring him, she pressed the button and waited.

Standing a little behind her, John looked her up and down. He knew every curve of her body, and as he studied her carefully he felt the desire rising within him. She'd always had this affect on him from the first moment he saw her, and even now, despite their differences, he still wanted her. His new girl was all right, she was a willing participant in their love-making, but she didn't have the fire that Connie had, and now, standing so close to her, it was driving him crazy.

The lift arrived, and the doors opened and they stepped inside. John leaned across her and pressed the button for the next floor, brushing her arms as he did so, which only inflamed him more.

'Good luck this morning, Connie,' he said. 'Don't be nervous, you'll be just fine.'

The sudden and unexpected kindness threw her. She smiled at him. 'Thank you.' It was just what she needed at that moment, and when she stepped out of the lift, she walked with an air of assurance.

The meeting went well. The overall takings of the store were up on the previous month, and the managing director noted that this was especially noticeable in haberdashery ever since Miss Morgan had taken over the buying.

'Good work, young lady. Keep it up!' He nodded in Connie's direction. She was elated.

Several people came down in the lift with Connie, but John Baker had taken the stairs rather than wait, so as Connie arrived at her counter, he walked over.

'Well done, Connie. I told you you'd be fine. Congratulations!' He walked away as Connie's friend Betty ambled over.

She was frowning and asked, 'What the hell did he want? Don't tell me he's sniffing around you again!'

To her surprise Connie found herself defending him. 'No, he wasn't. The MD complimented me on the increase in sales since I took over and he was congratulating me, that's all.'

'Yeah! That's the first move. You watch your step. As far as you're concerned he's like a dog after a bitch on heat!'

She stomped away before Connie could answer. But as Connie arranged a display she thought about her friend's remarks. She didn't think that was John's intention, but whatever it was, she was only too grateful. He had given her a boost just when she needed it and helped her over the hurdle of her first meeting with the big boss.

Baker stood across the way watching Connie. She'd matured since they had parted. Today in the meeting she'd held her own when producing her figures and suggestions and he'd been proud of her. It just seemed a pity, now that he was free, that they were no longer together, and he began to wonder if he could change that. He'd have to give it some thought.

Nineteen

Kay Baker was enjoying her freedom. She was happy with her job, which brought her in some mad money, as she called it – and she had an ardent lover. Edward was thoughtful and considerate in bed, and although John had been more than proficient between the sheets, with Edward she felt cosseted and loved. Now her divorce was complete, they were able to meet openly, and Kay had accompanied him to many official dinners. She knew that people were wondering if she was the woman that, after so long, Edward would choose as his wife. Kay let herself imagine such a role from time to time, but she was enjoying being single after so many years and as yet wasn't prepared to lose that position.

Edward, however, had decided that she was the woman he wanted to spend the rest of his life with and was working to that end, despite the problems he was having at work. His position within the Southampton Council was becoming untenable since the debacle over the building which had to be destroyed, and although no blame could be laid at his feet, several of the committee members had turned hostile towards his position and had insisted on an internal enquiry.

When he told Kay about this, she was outraged. 'They can't possibly think you had anything to do with it. Haven't the police had any results from their enquiries?'

'I'm afraid not. The man they want to question has gone to ground and as yet they've been unable to trace him.'

'That committee is full of old codgers!'

He laughed. 'What a delightful old-fashioned phrase. I can understand them in as far as the cost is concerned, but to be honest I did expect them to be more supportive. But there you are. They needed a whipping boy, and I was it.'

'They were worried the blame would be pointed in their direction, that's why.'

He pulled her closer. 'I'm really touched, Kay darling, that you are so defensive on my part.'

'Of course I am! I care about you.'

He tilted her chin and looked into her eyes, eyes that were bright with anger. 'It's been a very long time since anyone said that to me. How much *do* you care, Kay?'

'A very great deal,' she said softly and kissed him.

'Enough to make our relationship permanent?'

She gazed lovingly at him. Yes, nothing would please her more than to be Mrs Edward Harrington, but not just yet. It was too soon. She enjoyed not having to answer to a man, to be able to please herself. To be her own woman was so very good.

'I do care for you, Edward, and at some time in the future, ask me again, but I'm not ready just yet.'

He leaned forward and kissed her cheek. 'I do understand, darling. You've only just attained your freedom, which must be a great feeling, but I do love you. Try not to make me wait too long.'

It was by sheer chance that the police found the man they'd been looking for, who was the missing link in the fraud involving the building materials for Edward's new offices. Stan Bates had sneaked back to his home in Southampton one night and had been spotted by a sharp-eyed constable, who, recognizing him from the wanted board in the police station, had stopped him. The man tried to bluff his way out of being arrested but was eventually taken to the station to be questioned.

Several hours later, he eventually confessed and offered up the names of Gerry Cooper and Jake Barton as his associates in the crime. Both men were arrested, taken to the station and put in separate cells to wait until they were called to an interview room for questioning.

Jake Barton walked up and down the small

room, furious at being apprehended. He guessed that the man at the store had been caught because he knew that Gerry would have kept quiet. He had too much to lose. He already had a record so certainly wouldn't have been to the police. There was no other explanation.

When Gerry was questioned by the detective in charge of the case, he denied all knowledge of any wrongdoing, saying he was just the messenger, taking the invoice for goods to the supplier and collecting them for delivery. He wasn't to know there was any discrepancy.

The detective gave a wry smile. 'You're wasting your breath,' he said. 'Your mate from the suppliers has coughed the lot, so don't waste my time, sunshine. I've got you by the short and curlies! You both got forty per cent of the profit and Barton twenty.'

Cooper realized he was wasting his time arguing and gave a shrug.

Looking puzzled, the detective asked, 'Why did Barton get paid?'

'He was Mr Harrington's driver and used to go to all the building sites with him. He was to watch him closely in case he cottoned on to what was happening and could warn us.'

The policeman glared at Gerry. 'Do you realize that had this fraud not been discovered, the building would not have been safe? Lives were put at risk because of your greed. The judge won't look kindly on that.' He paused. 'Still, it won't be the first time you've been inside, will it?'

Gerry didn't answer.

Jake Barton sat at the table in the interview room and stared belligerently at the detective, who stared back at him without blinking.

'Well, Barton, you were always an accident waiting to happen! You make a habit of putting lives at risk on the racetrack, so being part of a dodgy build would have seemed small fry to you, no doubt.'

'Don't know what you're talking about!' Jake snapped.

'No, of course you don't. You had no idea that Stan Bates and Gerry Cooper were swapping cheaper inferior materials to give to the builders of the council offices and creaming the profit off the top, sharing it between the three of you.'

Barton's expression didn't change. 'I never had anything to do with the building materials. I was Mr Harrington's driver, that's all.'

'That's very true. You went to all the building sites with him, didn't you?'

'That's right.'

'By so doing, you could monitor his movements and would be on the spot had he noticed any discrepancies.'

Barton's eyes narrowed, but he remained silent.

'Had he done so, you were in the position to warn your partners in crime and they could have scarpered! Leaving you in the clear, because you were just a mouthpiece in this whole sad episode. No one would have tied you in as you had nothing to do with the buying of the materials. Neat! Very neat.'

Jake smirked. 'Prove it!'

Detective Inspector Glover sat back in the chair and grinned. 'Oh, I can ... without a doubt. Your two mates have coughed to the lot, and both have implicated you, Barton.'

Jake paled but remained calm. 'It's their word against mine!'

'True. It will be up to the judge and jury to decide who they believe. But remember, Barton, your reputation is hardly lily white. You were banned from the racetrack for six months due to your dangerous driving, putting others at risk. That won't go down well, and the prosecutor will certainly bring it up, to show what sort of a character you are!'

Jake lost his cool. 'This is a bloody fit-up!'

DI Glover laughed. 'Don't try and pull that old chestnut, Barton. You were given twenty per cent of the profit for being the lookout!'

There was silence in the room. Jake Barton's mind was working away, going over everything and wondering if he had any chance of getting away with his part. Well, he wasn't going to admit to anything and would take his chances by denying everything.

'I have no idea what you're talking about,' he said.

'Take him back to his cell,' the detective told the constable standing by the door. Turning to Barton he said, 'Get used to it, Barton, because you'll be in one for some time.'

The news of the arrests was a great relief to Edward Harrington, who took great pleasure in informing the council committee of the event. He cast a disparaging look around the men seated at the table.

'Well, gentlemen, there will no longer be the need of an internal enquiry now!'

One or two of them looked somewhat shamefaced and muttered about having to get to the bottom of the problem because of the finances involved.

'I quite understand that,' Edward said with a slow smile, 'however, I did not appreciate the insinuation that I had something to do with it!'

Being caught on the back foot, the men flushed and wriggled in their seats but remained silent.

Edward did not. 'Without the confidence of this committee I cannot continue in my present position so I am tendering my resignation!'

This completely floored them. Edward Harrington was good at his job, and they didn't want to lose him.

The chairman spoke. 'Edward, please reconsider. We were in a difficult position; surely you can understand that?'

'Oh, I do. But now consider mine. You doubted my integrity, my professionalism. That was unforgivable!' He rose from his seat. 'Good day, gentlemen!' Picking up his papers, he walked out of the room, smiling to himself as he listened to the raised voices behind him.

When he returned to his office he picked up the telephone and rang Kay's office.

'Kay Baker.'

'Hello, darling, can you get your mother to look after Susan for the weekend so we can go away? I feel the need of a break.'

There was something in his voice that made her feel that something was amiss. 'Yes, I'm sure that can be arranged,' she said carefully, aware that her conversation could be overheard.

'Good, I'll pop in tonight after work.'

Kay opened the door, kissed Edward on the cheek and said, 'Come into the kitchen. Susan's just had her supper. Would you like me to make you a drink of some kind?'

236

'I would kill for a cup of tea.'

She chuckled. 'Oh, you don't have to go that far.'

Edward sat beside Susan. 'Well, young lady, and how are you today?'

She looked at him and smiled. 'I'm fine. We did drawing today!' She held up a sheet of paper to show him.

He looked up at Kay and raised his eyebrows asking for help as he failed to recognize what had been drawn. She just shrugged.

'This is really good,' he said, studying it carefully. 'I like all the colours.'

'It's my house and that–' she pointed to a large blob in the middle – 'is me and my dog.'

'I didn't know you had a dog.'

'I don't really, silly, but I do in my picture. Can you draw?'

'A bit,' he said, keeping a straight face.

Susan handed him a clean piece of paper. 'Will you draw a house for me?'

'Of course, but first you must tell me what sort of house you'd like.'

Kay watched with great fascination as the two of them were in serious conversation as Edward started to draw. Considering that he was a bachelor, she was amazed at the natural way he handled her small daughter. It was the first time they'd sat together and talked for any length of time. She was fascinated. At last the drawing was finished and a delighted child held out the paper for her to see.

'Look, Mummy, at what Edward's drawn. It's beautiful!'

Kay looked at the thatched cottage, with curtains at the window, smoke coming from the chimney, roses growing round the door. A child and a dog were playing on the grass in the small garden.

'That's me and my dog!' Susan explained. But Kay didn't need to be told, the likeness was so good. She looked at Edward in surprise.

He laughed at her expression. 'I can draw other things than buildings,' he said.

'So it would seem. You never fail to surprise me.'

'I have another surprise. Today I resigned from the council.'

'Good heavens! What will you do now?'

He stared at her. 'That all depends on you, Kay.'

Twenty

Gerry Cooper, Stan Bates and Jake Barton were in court the following morning. They stood side by side in the dock and gave their names and addresses. Cooper and Bates were held on remand and Barton was released on bail until the trial was set.

As he walked away from the court, Jake couldn't believe his luck. He'd been warned not to leave Southampton or a warrant would be issued for his arrest. He wasn't a fool. He knew if he left it would be a sign of his guilt and he was convinced that if he continued to proclaim his innocence, there was a chance he could get away with it. Besides, there was another race he'd entered in a week's time and he didn't want to miss that.

But as the day progressed he had to face the fact that the jury might just believe his two associates and he could be charged and have to serve time in jail. That would put paid to his racing career altogether. If that *was* the case, he wanted to finish as a winner. The one person standing in his way was Sam Knight. Well, he'd have to see about that!

Kay Baker took Susan to school, then went

for a walk to try and gather her thoughts. She needed to make a decision that would affect the rest of her life and that of her daughter. She sat on a park bench, going over her conversation of the previous evening with Edward. He'd dropped a bombshell when he told her he'd resigned his position. When she'd asked him what his plans for the future were, he'd surprised her yet again.

'That depends on you, Kay,' he told her.

'What ever do you mean?'

'I've been offered a position that is too good to turn down, and if I'm honest I don't want to. But it will mean going to live in Paris for a year.'

'Paris?' She was shocked.

He took hold of her hand. 'Yes, Paris. Have you ever been there?'

'No.'

'I would like to take you and Susan with me.'

She frowned. 'I don't understand.'

He chuckled as he saw the consternation in her expression. 'Kay, darling, I'm asking you to marry me and come to Paris as my wife.'

Her knees seemed to give way beneath her, and she quickly sat down.

Edward started laughing. 'Well, honestly! Can it be such a terrible thing? You have gone quite pale at the thought! That's not exactly flattering, you know.'

She had to smile. This lovely man was offering to share his life with her and Susan and she'd reacted very badly.

'I'm sorry, Edward, but you took me by surprise. I don't know what to say.'

'Yes would be good!'

'When do you have to go?'

'Three months' time. But I'll have to go over there before to verify everything and sign a contract ... and if you agree to come with me, I'll have to find us somewhere to live and a school for Susan.'

She was very touched to think he'd considered Susan as well. But there was so much to be settled before she could say yes.

'I'd have to talk to John about taking Susan abroad. I do have full custody of her, but I would probably need his permission to do this.'

'We'll have a word with your solicitor first to see what the procedure is.'

She gazed fondly at him. 'Are you sure that taking my daughter too is what you want? You know we come as a package?'

He pulled her off the chair and held her. 'You are everything I want, and Susan too. She's a delightful child, and I always knew she would be part of our lives if ever you did me the honour of becoming my wife.' He kissed her longingly. 'Oh, Kay, the three of us could have such a wonderful life together, don't you agree?'

'Yes, I do, Edward, but please, this is such a big decision, give me time to think about it.'

For the first time since she'd known him, Edward looked uncertain. But he recovered quickly.

'Of course. I'm sorry, I know this came out of the blue but circumstances forced my hand. Normally I'd have given you all the time you needed. But will you come away this weekend no matter what?'

'Yes, of course I will.'

'Good. I'll pick you up on Saturday morning and bring you home on Monday if that's all right.'

She leaned forward and kissed him. 'That will be lovely.'

He had left and she was still in a whirl. Now she got to her feet and walked out of the house and headed for her mother's home.

'What do you mean you don't know what to do?'

Kay was sitting in her mother's kitchen after telling her what had transpired.

'Are you completely mad? For God's sake, Kay, you meet this wonderful man who adores you. He's willing to take you and your child. He's in a position to give you a good life, and you hesitate! I don't understand you at all. Especially after all you've been through with John. This man wouldn't be unfaithful to you, he's too honourable for that... Aren't you in love with him? Is that it?'

'Yes, I am in love with him. You've met him, why wouldn't I be?'

Her mother looked at her. 'Then what are you afraid of, for goodness' sake?'

'Nothing really, but it's all been so sudden.'

Her mother shook her head. 'You listen to me. A woman with a child is a lot for a man to take on, but he didn't hesitate. He must really love you to do that. If you lose him, you'll regret it for the rest of your life.'

'He wants the two of us to go away this weekend from Saturday until Monday.'

'Wonderful! It's just what you need. You go and before you come back you tell him you want to be part of his life. Good God! Give me a chance to live in Paris for a year with such a man and I'd be off like a shot!'

Kay started laughing. 'I do believe you would. What about dear old Dad?'

Her mother laughed too. 'Well, it's hardly likely to happen to me, which perhaps is just as well.'

Kay collected her things. 'Thanks, Mum. I just needed someone to give me a kick up the backside.' She kissed her on the cheek. 'I'll bring Susan over on Friday night after school.'

The weekend in Bath was blissful. Edward didn't mention the future at all, so Kay wasn't under any pressure. They spent time

243

exploring the beautiful city, wined, dined – and made love. It was the longest time they'd spent together, and Kay enjoyed every moment.

Edward was such good company. His knowledge of architecture made the trip even more interesting. And he made her laugh. As they walked hand in hand, she realized it had been years since she'd been so happy and asked herself why on earth she'd been so reticent about accepting his proposal.

On their last day, after a night of great sex, she held him close and staring into his eyes she spoke softly. 'Darling Mr Harrington, if you still want me, I'd love to share your life with you.'

He was both surprised and delighted. He gently stroked her naked body. 'Oh, Kay, darling, you've made me very happy. I know I've forced you into making a decision but I promise you will never regret it. Whilst I have breath in my body I will love you ... and Susan.'

On her return, Kay rang her ex-husband and asked him to come to the house as she wanted to talk to him.

John Baker was puzzled. Since their divorce, Kay had been very cool whenever he called at the house to collect Susan on the weekends when he was allowed to take her out. What on earth did Kay want? Could she possibly have had a change of heart? She certainly sounded different.

He stood on the doorstep of his old home, clutching an extravagant bouquet of flowers and rang the bell.

'Hello, John, please come in.' She led him into the sitting room.

He handed her the flowers.

'Thank you, they're lovely.'

He smiled and said, 'You're looking very well. I love the dress.' He sat on the settee wondering if she would sit beside him.

Kay sat on an armchair opposite him. 'Thank you for coming. There's something I want to tell you.'

He leaned nonchalantly back in his seat and waited.

'I'm getting married,' said Kay.

He sat up, shocked at the statement. 'You what?'

Kay looked at the expression on his face and hid a smile. My goodness, he looks outraged, she thought, then she wondered if for one moment he'd had the audacity to think she wanted him back. Knowing him so well, she realized that was precisely what he'd been thinking.

'What do you mean you're getting married? Christ, Kay! We've only just been divorced!'

'I know but circumstances are such that I've had to make a quick decision.'

'Who is this man, may I ask?'

'I'm going to marry Edward Harrington, the architect.'

He was stunned into silence.

'But there is something more. When we are married, we'll be living in Paris for a year.'

'Paris?' This was all too much to take in. 'But – but what about Susan?' he stuttered.

'That's what we need to discuss. Of course Susan will come with us. Edward is already looking for a suitable school. I'm sure you'll think this will be an excellent opportunity for her.'

His nostrils flared with anger. 'You can't possibly think I'd be happy about this? What about the weekends we spend together? Those times mean everything to me. I'll never see her if you take her away!'

Aware that the one thing he was genuine about was the love he had for his daughter, Kay trod carefully.

'I know this is asking a lot of you, John, and it isn't an ideal situation, but I don't have a choice. Edward will be working there, and as his wife, I want to be with him, and where I go, so does Susan.'

'Not if I object!'

'You'll be able to have her during the school holidays. I'll bring her home.'

John Baker was in a quandary. Firstly, he was shocked that Kay was getting married. He'd always believed that eventually they would get back together, and now it was obvious this wasn't going to happen. This was a serious blow to his ego. He'd always held the upper hand as far as his women went. He was the one who always made the decisions, and he was not happy that another man was making plans for *his* daughter. This was unthinkable!

He stood up. 'No, I'm sorry, Kay, but you and your boyfriend will have to rethink your plans. My daughter isn't going anywhere!'

As he walked to the door, Kay followed him. 'In that case I'll see you in court!'

He stopped suddenly and turning said, 'What? What on earth do you mean?'

'If you won't be reasonable, we have no choice but to let a court decide Susan's future.' She stared coldly at him. 'This is not the way I want things, John. I'll give you twenty-four hours to reconsider. I know this has been a shock to you, it's been rather a surprise to me, but Edward will be leaving in three months' time and by then we'll be married.'

At a loss for words, he opened the door and left the house.

It was Connie's habit to walk along to the Tudor Cafe during her lunch break for a snack. She'd just ordered a sandwich and a coffee when to her surprise John Baker walked in and, coming over to her table, asked if he could join her. She was about to refuse until she saw the pallor of his face. She nodded her approval.

'Are you all right?' she asked.

'No, I'm not. I saw Kay yesterday and she told me she was getting married!'

Connie's first thought was *gracious, that's quick*. The divorce hadn't been finalized for that long. But she could see that her ex-lover was shaken by the news.

'Who's she marrying?'

'Edward Harrington.'

Connie didn't know the man but there had been an article in the local paper recently about his resignation – and a picture of him. She'd thought he was very good-looking, but realized it would be unkind to say so and kept silent.

'And what's more they are going to live in Paris for a year.'

'How lovely,' she said without thinking. 'I would love to do that.'

He glared at her. 'They want to take Susan with them!'

She then realized why he looked so drawn. 'Paris isn't that far away, John. It's not as if they are going to the ends of the earth.'

'I don't care, I just can't allow it!' He then went into a long tirade about the situation.

She tried to reason with him. 'I know this isn't perhaps what you expected but surely you must have realized that Kay getting married again was a possibility, as it is for you.'

'What do you mean?'

'To be honest I can't see you going through life alone. One day you'll meet someone you'll want to settle down with.'

'This isn't about marriage, this is about my daughter!'

'I can see you're unhappy about this, John, but you sound like the victim here and you're not! Had you been a good husband the whole scenario would be different!'

He glared at her. 'That's shoving the knife in, Connie. How could you?'

'Because it's the truth! I know you love Susan, but do you have the right to interfere with her future? After all I'm sure you'll be able to see her at some time.'

'Only in school holidays!'

'Think how wonderful that'll be. You could take a holiday in Paris and explore the city together. That would be nice for both of you. After all, how could you take care of her? You work all day. You wouldn't be able to meet her from school, make her tea. She needs to be with her mother. Surely you can see that?'

She drank her coffee, wrapped her sandwich in a paper napkin and rose to her feet. 'Think about Susan, John, and stop thinking about yourself for once!'

As she walked back to the store she thought *good for you, Kay Baker! I hope you'll be very happy!* If all went well, in the future she would be Mrs Sam Knight. How ironic. Two of John's women, marrying other people, leaving him to lick his wounds. That had to be some kind of justice.

Twenty-One

It was race day and Sam and his friends were full of hope. The car had been thoroughly tested and was ready two days beforehand which had given the three men a bit of breathing space before the big day. It had also allowed Sam to rest up, as this race was long and arduous. For once they hadn't needed to work on the vehicle up until the last moment and it had stood in the garage in Shirley, ready and waiting.

It was a Sunday meeting so Connie had been able to accompany Sam to Brands Hatch to watch. She stood by as the drivers climbed into their cars and drove to the starting line. Jake Barton drew up beside Sam as he was climbing into his car.

'Today is mine, Knight!' he said with a sneer. 'You don't stand a chance.'

Sam just grinned at him. 'We'll see,' he said and started the engine.

Connie overhead the comment, but there was something about Barton's attitude that chilled her. Whenever this man was in the same race as Sam, it filled her with foreboding, but never as much as today. She looked at Tom.

Sensing her dismay he said, 'Don't you take no notice of him, love. He's full of bull!'

But as she watched them drive away, her stomach tightened with apprehension.

The race began. The noise was almost overwhelming as each lap was driven flat out, drivers jockeying for position. She had to admit that Jake Barton was driving well. He and Sam were moving up the field with each lap, always within a car or two of each other, until there were just four laps to go.

Sam was aware that Jake was on his tail and creeping up slowly until he was just behind him as he approached the most dangerous corner on the track. Sam put his foot on the brake ready to drop down a gear but his foot went straight to the floor. There was no traction at all. He pumped the brake, but to no avail, and he was heading for the corner at speed. There was no way he was going to make it, and he knew it. The car hit a pile of tyres and spun, then it flew into the air, turning over and over, before it crashed into a barrier, thankfully clear of the spectators and the track. Barton drove past, laughing loudly.

Connie screamed when she saw the car crash. Tom grabbed her as she made to rush over to the spot. 'You stay put, girl, and wait a bit or you'll get yourself killed!' The other cars rushed by.

They both waited hoping to see Sam climb out of the vehicle, but all they saw were the stewards, using their fire extinguishers, pre-empting a fire. Then they saw them lifting Sam gingerly out of the driver's seat and putting him on a stretcher, and then he was carried to an ambulance, which, as always, was standing by.

Both Tom and Connie ran, pushing their way through the crowds, leaving Harry to see to the car. They got there just in time to allow the two of them to go with the ambulance to the hospital.

A paramedic was holding a mask over Sam's face, whilst another man was checking his vital signs.

'Is he going to be all right?' Connie asked, hardly daring to breathe.

'We won't know until we get him to the hospital,' he said.

Once they arrived, Sam was rushed to the operating theatre, and Connie and Tom were told to wait.

'What could have happened?' asked Connie, her voice filled with despair.

Tom looked puzzled. 'I can't imagine. Sam drove into the corner far too fast. That's not like him at all; he would have braked, changed gear and *then* put his foot down. I don't understand it at all.'

Three hours later, the surgeon emerged from the operating theatre and walked towards them. They both got to their feet and waited.

'Mr Knight is going to be all right, eventually,' were his first words.

Connie thought she was going to faint with relief.

'However,' continued the surgeon, 'he did sustain some serious injuries. One of his legs is broken, his pelvis and two of his ribs. He dislocated his shoulder, and he's concussed. I'm afraid he won't be racing again for some considerable time.'

'Can we see him?' asked Connie.

'Not now, miss. He still hasn't come round from the anaesthetic. Come back this evening.'

Outside they took a taxi back to the circuit. Harry was waiting for them, the tangled remains of the car loaded on the truck. Connie looked at the wreck and thought how lucky Sam was to have come out of it alive.

Harry immediately asked for the latest news and listened carefully to what was said. 'Thank God for that. Once we've got the car home we'll take it to pieces and examine it closely because no way would Sam have taken that corner at that speed, unless he had no choice!'

'You think there was a mechanical fault?' asked Tom.

'No, I don't! We both know the car was mechanically sound, but it was in the garage for two days. Maybe someone got to it.'

'Oh my God!' Tom was shaken. 'I was so

shocked to see Sam crash, I didn't have time to think.' He paused. 'Who won the race?'

'Jake Barton.' Harry stared at his mate. 'Now that makes me very suspicious. Remember how he baited Sam before the race? He never does that, he always keeps well away. It's almost as if he knew something was going to happen.'

'If that's the case, we'll never be able to prove it,' said Tom.

'Well, we'll check the car first before we jump to conclusions,' was Harry's advice.

That evening, Connie and Tom returned to the hospital, hoping to see Sam. They were told they could only stay a few minutes and they were not to tire the patient.

Connie smothered a cry when she saw Sam, covered in bandages and his leg in plaster. He looked pale and drawn as he gave a wan smile as they entered his room.

Connie took his hand and leaned forward to kiss him, making sure she didn't put any pressure on his injured body. 'Hello, darling.'

Tom stood beside her. 'Hello, mate! You gave us all a bloody fright, I can tell you. What happened?'

In a voice that was barely audible Sam whispered, 'No brakes. My foot went to the floor.'

Just then a nurse came in and told them they'd have to leave. 'I'll be back tomorrow,

Sam,' said Tom. 'You take care.' He walked away to give Connie a moment alone.

Trying to be calm for her lover's sake, Connie kissed him softly and said, 'As soon as we can we'll have you moved back to Southampton, and when you come out of hospital I'll kill you with kindness.'

'I'd like that,' he said. 'But don't you worry, darling, I'll be fine.'

But as Connie walked down the corridor with Tom, she wondered just how long it would take for Sam to recover.

Tom, however, was deep in thought and was silently seething. He knew something had to be wrong for Sam to have made such a mistake on that corner. He was too good a driver for that. There was no doubt in his mind that Jake Barton was behind it, but how could they prove it?

Three days later Sam was moved down to the South Hants Hospital, in Southampton, which made it easier for Connie and Sam's friends and family to visit. But it became obvious that the recovery time would take months.

In the garage, Tom, Harry and young Jimmy started the arduous task of sifting through the wreckage, trying to locate the fault in the brakes.

The local paper had been full of Sam's crash and the injuries he'd sustained, sympathizing with the fact that this popular driver would be incapacitated for months ahead and wondering if he'd ever race again. There had been no mention at all of Barton's win. No photographs of him holding the trophy.

John Baker had also read the article. Having watched Sam race and recognizing his talent, he did feel sympathetic. Had Sam not been Connie's boyfriend he would have liked to have known him better. He had his own problems, however. He'd been to his solicitor to get advice about contesting the custody of his daughter, but his solicitor had advised against it.

'The court will uphold the mother's right,' he said. 'She will be free to care for Susan, whereas you work and would have to employ a nanny. The court will say the child should remain with the mother. She's offered to let you have Susan during the school holidays, so she's not being difficult.'

Baker eventually had to accept his advice, as he was told it would be wasted money to take such a case to court. He reluctantly rang Kay and agreed to her demands.

The following day he walked over to Connie's counter, which was without any customers at that moment, and said how sorry he was to read of Sam Knight's accident.

Connie was taken by surprise. 'Thank you, John. He's coming along well, but of course when he'll be able to race again is still in doubt.' Knowing his situation she asked, 'How are things with you?'

He looked crestfallen. 'Susan will go to Paris with her mother and her mother's new husband when they marry,' he said. 'I'm not happy about it but I don't have much choice.' He gazed at her and said, 'We have both had a rough time. Perhaps we could get together for a drink and commiserate with each other?'

'I don't think that's a good idea,' she said.

'I don't see why not. We both need a bit of comfort at the moment, we could help each other through the rough times.'

'What game are you playing now, John? Do you think I'm in such a state I'll come rushing back into your arms, is that it?'

From his enigmatic smile she knew that was just what he was thinking. 'You will never understand me. I love Sam, and even if we were to part, I'd never run back to you. Now leave me alone.' She walked away.

Kay Baker was rushing around like a demented flee, trying to prepare for her forthcoming wedding. Edward spent several days in Paris on business, looking for somewhere to live and searching for a school for Susan. That evening he was due home and Kay was preparing dinner after bathing Susan and putting her to bed.

When she opened the door, she could see

258

how tired Edward was. She kissed him and ushered him into the kitchen and poured him a gin and tonic. 'You look as if you need this, darling.'

He rubbed his eyes. 'Thanks, it has been somewhat hectic,' he said and sat down on a stool. 'However, I've found us a nice apartment overlooking the Seine and a school for Susan. It's an International one using the English curriculum so the teachers all speak English. She'll learn French, of course.'

'Come into the sitting room and tell me all about it,' she suggested.

They sat on a settee, and he gave her all the details. 'On the plane I wondered just what we should do about this house,' he said.

'What do you mean?'

'Well, when eventually we come home from Paris we'll move into mine, and for a year this will be empty, which is never a good idea.'

'To be honest I've been too busy to think about it.'

'If you're agreeable, of course, I thought it would be a good idea to let your ex have it. After all, it was his home, and we don't need it, do we?'

Kay looked at him and stroked his cheek. 'Edward, you are such a kind man. I think that's a wonderful idea. It will help John to get over us taking Susan away. He loves this house, so perhaps he'll be a bit happier moving back in, and when Susan comes back to stay with him it will be somewhere she's familiar with. Any precious things I want, I can take with me. I can't think he'd mind.'

Jake Barton was in a foul mood. There had been another article in the paper reporting the latest news of Sam Knight's recovery and still none of Barton's win, which really stuck in his craw. He knew that Knight's girlfriend worked and would be unable to visit the patient during the day, and he was also aware that Tom and Harry were dismantling the wrecked car during daylight hours, so he went to the South Hants Hospital and asked which ward Sam was in.

The receptionist smiled at him and asked, 'Are you a relative?'

'No, I'm a friend ... another racing driver. Just want to see how he's making out.'

She seemed very impressed. 'Mr Knight is in a private room,' she said and told him where to go.

As he made his way along the hospital corridors, he fumed. 'Bleeding private room too. Treating him like some bloody hero!'

When he arrived at the room and read the name on the door, he looked around, but there were only hospital staff going about their business. He turned the handle and walked in.

Sam looked at his visitor with surprise.

Jake stood inside the door and studied the patient. The bandaged shoulder, arm in a sling, the leg encased in plaster, and he started to laugh.

'Not exactly the conquering hero now, are you?'

Sam glowered at him. 'What do you want, Barton?'

Jake walked slowly over to the bed. 'I told you, you didn't stand a chance in that race didn't I? You should have listened.'

'You fixed my brakes, you bastard! You could have killed me!'

'Nah! That would have been murder. I knew you had enough skill to get you out of trouble, but you went into the corner faster than I envisaged. That was your fault, not mine.'

'It wouldn't have been if my brakes had been working!' Sam was flushed with anger. He wanted to hit out at his rival. Teach him a lesson – but he could hardly move. 'Get out, Barton! When I'm on my feet I'll have you. You won't get away with this.'

'I'll send you a picture of me holding the trophy. That'll cheer you up! You take care now ... loser!'

Twenty-Two

The mystery of the failing brakes had been solved by Tom and Harry who, sifting through the remains of the damaged car, found that minute holes had been drilled in the bottom of the reservoir holding the brake fluid. This would have slowly seeped out until eventually the brakes failed.

The men knew who was responsible but there was no way of proving it, so there was little point in going to the police. Even if Sam had told them of his conversation with Jake, Jake would have denied it – but it infuriated all of them.

'What really pisses me off,' said Tom as he and Harry sat at Sam's bedside, 'is the fact that he'll get away with it!'

'Well, remember he's up in court shortly on this fraud charge. Maybe he'll be sent down for that. At least that would be something!'

'But he's out on bail,' retorted Harry. 'The other two are on remand, which makes me wonder if they have enough evidence to convict him.'

'We'll just have to wait and see,' said Sam. 'But I intend to be in that court room when the case comes up, to see for myself.'

'Apparently, that won't be for another couple of months,' Tom told him.

'Good, that gives me time to get back on my feet.'

During that time, Kay Baker had been preparing for her wedding. It was to be a fairly quiet affair, with a reception after at the Polygon Hotel. With Kay having been divorced, the ceremony was to take place at the registry office. But, as she told Edward, she'd had the church wedding, and look where that had ended!

'I'm only sorry we won't have time for a honeymoon,' he said. 'But when Susan comes back here to spend time with her father during the school holidays, perhaps then we can go somewhere?'

She entwined her arms around his neck and kissed him. 'It isn't important. As long as we're together, it doesn't matter where we are.'

'Darling Kay, you're so easy to please, I'm going to enjoy spoiling you.'

She gazed at the man with whom she was to share her life, unable to believe how lucky she was. She had no regrets about getting her divorce. She was certain that Edward would always stand by her and Susan. They would have a better life in every way. Susan and Edward got along so well, and she knew that he would also be a good influence on the life of her daughter.

John had been surprised when she'd asked him to the house to tell him she'd be handing him the keys before she left.

'What do you mean?' he'd asked.

'We no longer need the house,' she explained. 'We'll be away for a year, and when we return, we'll go and live with Edward. He thought it only fair that you should come back here.'

He should have been delighted but the fact that the idea came from the man Kay was going to marry infuriated him.

'How kind of him to return something that was mine in the first place!'

Kay looked at the spiteful line of John's mouth. 'Stop behaving like a child who's thrown his toys out of the pram! I could have let the house for a year and you couldn't have done a thing about it. At least have the decency to be thankful you'll have your own roof over your head and have Susan living in a place she's familiar with when she comes to stay with you.'

'Well, Kay, I must say you've done well for yourself. Harrington can give you a better way of life than I ever could have.'

She hated his churlish manner. 'In every way, John – in *every* way! I'll never have to worry whose bed he's in because it will always be mine!'

They had not parted amicably.

The local press were outside the registry office, waiting for the bride to arrive, having already taken pictures of the groom and his best man, when a car draped in wedding ribbons drove up.

Out stepped David, Kay's father, who turned to help the bride, who was dressed in a pale green suit with matching shoes, a cream hat and gloves, followed by Susan, in a pale primrose dress and matching ribbon in her hair. They stood whilst the press took pictures before walking into the registry office.

'Will we be in the paper, Mummy?' asked her excited daughter.

'Yes, darling, we will. Now you must be quiet until the ceremony is over.'

Later, Edward Harrington and his bride stood greeting their guests for the reception at the Polygon Hotel. There were many notable people attending. Associates and friends of the groom and friends of the bride and her family.

Kay's parents arrived. Her mother grinned broadly at her daughter and kissed her.

'I am so very happy for you, Kay darling. This time you've picked a winner. Be happy!'

The meal was sumptuous, with good wine and champagne. The best man made an amusing speech and read out the telegrams, then Edward got to his feet.

'Ladies and gentleman, you see before you the happiest man in Britain because today I married a beautiful woman who was brave enough to accept my proposal of marriage – and those who thought I'd remain a bachelor can perhaps now understand why I waited so long!' There was a ripple of laughter around the room.

'But I don't just have one beautiful woman in my life now. Susan, Kay's lovely daughter, is now part of my family also. What more can a man ask for?' He smiled over at Susan who grinned back at him.

'As you know, in a few days we will all be moving to Paris for a year, which is exciting for us all, but we will be back. Until then, thank you all for coming and sharing this very special day with us.'

He sat down and, leaning forward, kissed Kay. 'Hello, Mrs Harrington.'

Everybody cheered.

Two days later, Kay's parents saw the three of them off at the ferry taking them across the Channel to France. Susan was beside herself with excitement and was telling her grandparents about the trip.

'We're going to live in Paris, Nanny, and I'm to go to a new school. Edward said I'd like it ... and I'll be learning French!'

Seeing the tears glistening in the eyes of

his mother-in-law, Edward placed an arm around her shoulders. 'When we're settled, you must come and stay,' he said. 'I made sure to get an apartment with a spare room. Now, you're not to worry, we'll be fine.'

She hugged him. 'I know, I know. Good luck with the new job and take care.'

She and her husband waved them off as they drove on to the ferry.

Sam Knight was now out of hospital and back in business. Not that he was able to do a great deal physically as he was still using crutches to get around, but he had his first racing car to tune for another driver and he and his team were hard at work. That day in the garage, he was telling Connie all about it.

'This is a great car,' he said enthusiastically, 'and with the engine I built I know I can improve its performance, even more than the driver expects. I already have another to do when this is finished. The call came in this morning.' His eyes shone with delight.

'That's wonderful, Sam! When you've fully recovered will you go back to racing or will you now branch out into this new line of business? I know it was your ultimate dream.' She held her breath as she waited for his answer. After seeing him crash, she dreaded him returning to the race circuit.

He saw her worried expression and slowly drew her into his arms. 'You'd like that, wouldn't you, sweetheart?'

She wanted to yell, *'Yes! Yes!'* but she knew how much he loved racing. 'You have to do what's right for you, Sam, or you'll end up a frustrated old man.'

He looked at her and slowly shook his head. 'You hate seeing me race, but you'd still support my decision if I said I'd go back on the track, wouldn't you?'

She felt sick. 'Of course I would. I love you.'

He kissed the tip of her nose. 'Relax, sweetheart, I've decided to retire from racing.'

Connie burst into tears.

Both Tom and Harry emerged from the engine to see what was going on.

'It's all right, boys, everything's fine. I've just told Connie I will no longer be racing. You know women, they are such emotional creatures!'

He wiped away the tears trickling down her face. 'We are on our way, Connie darling. This is the start of something big. Once I've got this business established, we'll get married, then you won't have to work ... except at looking after me.'

'Perhaps I can help you in the business,' she suggested. 'I'm used to going to work; being at home all day will drive me mad. After all, how often can you clean a house?'

He thought for a moment. 'Well, if you feel that way, you could help with the paperwork, at least until we have children.'

She began to picture life as Mrs Sam Knight. How wonderful it would be. Especially now she knew she wouldn't have to worry about Sam racing, wondering if he would survive each race uninjured.

She hugged him. 'It all sounds wonderful.'

'And it will be, I promise.'

It was the first day of the trial and as Jake dressed he felt the tension in every bone in his body. He had met with his solicitor, declaring his innocence, lying convincingly, he thought. He didn't know if the solicitor believed him, but he knew that, no matter what, it was the man's job to try and get him off the charges made against him. He was arrogant enough to believe he could convince the judge and jury he'd had nothing to do with it.

The three men were led into the dock together, not speaking to each other. As he mounted the steps and stood in the dock, Jake looked round the court room and saw Sam Knight, his two mechanics and his girlfriend sitting among the visitors.

Sam gazed coldly at him.

The trial began with the prosecutor stating his case. He explained to the jury in detail how the men had ordered the wrong building materials and how they had kept the money they made and shared it between them. He also explained how dangerous this had been, with the building being unsafe due to the incorrect materials being used, and how the building had to be destroyed at great cost to the council.

Edward Harrington had returned from France to give evidence. He told the court how he'd noticed that the girders were not the ones he'd ordered and how, from that, the whole scam had been discovered. Then Edward's foreman gave his evidence. And so it went on until the judge called an end to the day's proceedings.

As Jake and the others were led away, Jake caught hold of Gerry Cooper's arm and, beneath his breath, he threatened him.

'You shop me and I'll get you, no matter how long it takes!'

Cooper shook off his hold and was led away to the cells to wait overnight.

The following day, Stan Bates, the man who'd worked in the suppliers and had worked the fraud with Gerry Cooper, took the stand. His hands shook as he took the oath.

The prosecutor rose to his feet. 'Mr Bates, I believe you have worked for Billings Brothers for a number of years, is that right?'

'Yes, sir, six years next February.'

'Have you ever been in trouble with the law before?'

'No, sir, never!'

'Would I be right in saying you are or were a trusted member of staff, who ran his department to the satisfaction of your employers during this time?'

'That I did, sir.'

'Then can you please explain why you suddenly changed from being a law-abiding member of society to one who stole from your employers?'

'Well, sir, it's like this. I started gambling and I got into debt. I was having a drink with Gerry Cooper one night, telling him I was in a load of trouble, and he suggested a way out, one which would allow me to pay me debts.'

'So it was Mr Cooper's suggestion?'

'Yes, sir. Nothing like that had ever entered my head before.'

'And what was your reply?'

'At first I refused, I was too scared, but I went gambling again and lost more money, so in the end I agreed. He said we'd never be found out.'

'Tell the jury how your scheme worked.'

Bates went into detail and explained how the two of them worked together exchanging inferior materials, yet still charging for the original items on the invoice and pocketing the surplus money.

'So the money was paid to you?'

'Yes, I was in charge of my department from beginning to end. Otherwise it wouldn't have worked.'

'What part did Jake Barton play in this?'

'He went round the sites with Mr Harrington so he was able to tell if his boss noticed anything wrong whilst walking round the site. If he did, he was to give us the nod.'

'Thank you, Mr Bates. No further questions.'

Bates's solicitor could do little after such damning evidence so he didn't ask any questions, apart from emphasizing Bates's statement that had it not been for Cooper's suggestion he would never have been involved.

Then Gerry Cooper was called to the stand.

The prosecutor stepped forward. 'Mr Cooper, unlike Mr Bates, you have been in trouble with the law, have you not?'

'Yes, sir, I have.' He stood listening whilst his past demeanours were read out. There were several cases of burglary, one of assault and another of being drunk and disorderly.

'And now you are being accused of fraud. What have you to say for yourself?'

'I was just trying to help out a friend, sir.'

There was laughter in the court.

With a wry smile the man in front of him said, 'Of course you were, and lining your own pockets at the same time. You didn't give a thought to how dangerous this was. You didn't for one moment think that you might have caused a dreadful tragedy when eventually the unsafe building would collapse, maybe injuring someone – or even worse?'

'No, sir, I did not! Had I known that I would never have even considered such a thing!'

'What *did* you think, may I ask?'

Cooper shrugged. 'I thought it was all right and the building was just being made much cheaper, that's all.'

'And you were convinced you'd be able to get away with it too.'

'I couldn't see no harm in it. It was just a way to make a bit of money on the side. Everybody has some sort of fiddle on the go. I bet you tell a few porkies when you do your tax returns.'

The judge banged his gavel to try and stop the noise of the laughter in the court.

'Order! Order!'

Trying to hide a smile the prosecutor said, 'No, I don't, Mr Cooper, that would be illegal! Tell me, how did Jake Barton become involved in your little scheme?'

'We was playing darts, and Jake was saying things were quiet, and I suggested a way he could make a bit of money on the side. Harrington needed a driver and that fitted into our plans.'

'And he was agreeable?'

'Absolutely! He never hesitated, and it was good for us to have a man on the inside, so to speak.'

'I have no more questions, your honour,' the prosecutor said, and he sat down.

Cooper's solicitor tried in vain to lighten the case against his client, stating his ignorance of the consequences of his actions, but it was hardly convincing.

Then Jake Barton was called to the witness stand. He took the oath and stood staring defiantly at the prosecutor, who rose to question him.

'So, Mr Jake Barton. You are a man not afraid to take a risk, as we know from the history of your car racing. Indeed, you have been warned about your dangerous driving several times, and recently you were banned from racing for six months, isn't that right?'

'You know it is; it isn't a secret!'

'This no doubt will have affected your income. After all, you earn the majority of your living this way.'

'I also have a garage and repair cars, which is my main living!' Jake retorted.

'Yet you gave that up to become Edward Harrington's driver, didn't you?'

'I did.'

'Now, Mr Barton, I suggest to you this was because, after being banned from the race-track, business was slack.'

'Yeah, it dropped off a bit.'

'We've already heard from Gerry Cooper that you agreed to be the lookout for him and his accomplice. What do you have to say to that?'

'I don't know what he's talking about. It's the first I've heard of it. I went for the job when I saw it advertised in the paper. All what he said is rubbish!'

There was a buzz of conversation at this.

'So you deny having anything to do with this hare-brained scheme?'

'First I knew was when I read about it in the paper.'

'Then can you explain to me why both these men have named you as an accomplice?'

'No, I can't. I used to play darts with Gerry Cooper but I've never met the man standing with him.' He pointed to the men in the dock.

The judge looked at his watch. 'I think, gentlemen, we'll leave things here for today and meet again tomorrow at ten o'clock.'

Twenty-Three

The following morning, the court room was full of spectators. Sam, his two men and Connie took their places and waited. The jury filed in and took their seats in readiness.

'All stand!' the clerk of the court demanded as the judge made his entrance.

Jake Barton was called back to the stand.

The prosecutor rose to his feet. 'Remember, Mr Barton, you're still under oath. Do you still deny that you had knowledge of the scheme that Mr Cooper and Mr Bates were involved with?'

'I do.'

'Tell the court again how you came to be employed as Mr Harrington's driver.'

'Business was slack, and I was looking at the situations vacant in the *Southern Evening Echo*. I saw an advert for a chauffeur and I applied.'

'In the situations vacant, you say?'

'Yes, sir.'

'What did you do then?'

'I wrote off a letter applying for the job.'

'Now, Mr Barton, I find that very strange, because the post was never advertised in any paper.'

Jake was taken aback by this, but he tried to bluff it out. 'Then you're mistaken, sir.'

'No, Mr Barton, I am not. Mr Harrington told me yesterday that this was so. I made my enquiries, and it seems that Mr Cooper knew of the vacancy and put in a word for you, then set up an interview which you attended. That's how you were employed as Mr Harrington's driver. You have been lying, Mr Barton. I suggest your whole story is a pack of lies, that indeed you *were* the inside man, and that you *did* receive twenty per cent of the money, as the others stated, for your part in this illegal scheme!'

Jake Barton paled. He had been found out and now knew he was in trouble.

The prosecutor carried on. 'I would suggest that it would be wiser to stop trying to fool the court and tell the truth.'

'All right! But I didn't know what the other two planned. All I knew was that I had to tell them if Mr Harrington started asking questions about the building materials. I didn't know why because I never asked.'

'Maybe so, but that makes you an accessory to the crime.'

Barton didn't reply.

'I have no further questions, your honour.'

Barton's defence lawyer tried to reiterate the fact that Barton was unaware of what was going on, but he couldn't deny the fact that his client was involved.

Sam turned to the others and whispered, 'They've got him!'

The two lawyers made their closing speeches, and the judge advised the jury before they left the courtroom to consider their verdict.

Sam and the others went outside to have a smoke whilst they waited.

Tom drew deeply on his cigarette. 'Will he go down, do you think?'

They were all wondering the same thing. Sam was the first to answer. 'I don't see how he can get away with it. After all, he aided and abetted them, that fact can't be denied. He probably won't get such a long sentence as the others, but he *has* to serve time, surely?'

The jury didn't take long to come to a decision and returned to the court room two hours later. They found both Gerry Cooper and Stan Bates guilty as charged and Jake Barton guilty of aiding and abetting.

The three men stood as the judge gave his sentence.

'You, Gerald Cooper, through your greed for money, consorted with Stanley Bates to commit a fraud which put innocent lives at risk. In so doing you have also caused considerable cost to the council, who had to pull down the building in question. You are fortunate, gentlemen, not to be standing before me on a far more serious charge. Whilst you are in prison, perhaps you will spend some time realizing how serious this could have been. I sentence you each to five years penal servitude.'

The two men each let out a gasp of horror.

He then looked at Jake Barton. 'As for you, Mr Barton, you lied on oath to try and save your neck, yet you are as guilty as the other two. I have taken into consideration that you may not have been aware of the details of their crime. Nevertheless, you aided and abetted them and for that you have to pay the price. You will serve two years in prison – and six months on top of that for lying on oath! Take them down.'

Sam was sitting close to the dock. As Jake was leaving he looked over towards Sam.

'Who's the loser now, Barton?' Sam said quietly.

Jake stopped and swore at him, but was shoved towards the steps by a policeman.

Outside Sam said, 'Come on, everyone, let's find a pub and celebrate!'

As they settled with their drinks, Sam remarked, 'Barton will find it hard inside.'

'How do you mean?' Tom asked.

'He doesn't take kindly to authority, he's a belligerent bugger, and I can only think he'll find it impossible to knuckle down to prison life. Cooper's been there already so will settle, but Stan Bates will find it hard. To lose your freedom is never easy, I wouldn't think.'

'They should have thought of that!' Connie retorted.

'I felt sorry for Edward Harrington, the architect,' Sam continued. 'I know if I built a new car and found out someone had messed with it, I'd be furious! After all, people might question my professionalism. But at least he's been exonerated.'

Connie remained silent. She'd liked the look of the architect as he gave his evidence and hoped that he and John Baker's ex-wife were now happy. The former Mrs Baker's new husband was so different from John. He looked more solid ... more of a gentleman.

Harry looked thoughtful. 'At least we're free of Jake Barton and his jealousy of you, Sam. When he gets out, his racing days are probably over.'

Sam gave a wry smile. 'So are mine! Stupid idiot, had he kept his nose clean, he might have had the chance of winning more times on the track.'

Jake Barton had never felt less like a winner, as once he'd been admitted to the prison with the others he'd been made to strip, had been bodily searched and made to shower, before being handed his prison clothes and bedding. By the time he was led away to his cell, he was seething. One of the warders took hold of his arm firmly as they made to walk along the corridor.

Barton jerked his arm away. 'I can manage without any help!'

The warder gave a look of disdain at his new prisoner. 'That attitude will only get you into trouble, Barton. You'd best calm down and do your time quietly.'

'Fuck off!' was the reply.

The warder unlocked the cell door and pushed him inside. 'You'll learn,' he said as he closed the door and locked it behind him.

Jake looked around the small room with its single bed, wash stand, wooden chair and bucket. He threw the bedclothes on the bed, lit a cigarette and sat down. *Two and a half bloody years in this place, all because I needed to make some extra money ... I'll never make it,* he thought.

During the following months, Sam's business flourished. Word soon spread of his exceptional ability, and he had so much work that he'd had to move to larger premises. Young Jimmy Murphy had now joined the team, to his great delight, and he'd become a considerable help.

Connie was enjoying her own success as head of her department, and as sales increased she was given a rise in salary. John

Baker was still working as floor manager, but now they just had a working relationship without any animosity, mainly because John had met a young woman who stood no nonsense from him. His divorce had shaken him, and he missed family life more than he cared to admit. He lived for the times when Susan was allowed to stay with him. This was not without its downside as he had to listen to her talk about Edward Harrington with such affection that he found it hard to tolerate. But he had to admit his daughter was happy and was doing well at school. Every time she had to leave to go back to France, though, he found it hard to bear.

Eventually, out of loneliness, he proposed marriage to his girlfriend and she accepted. When she became pregnant he was delighted and silently vowed that this time he wouldn't make the same mistake and lose another child.

When Kay heard the news of the pregnancy, she was happy for her ex-husband and sincerely hoped he'd learned his lesson, but deep down she felt doubtful. After so many years of infidelity, she doubted that he could change that much. She just hoped that he'd be as happy as she was. Edward was everything she'd hoped for. He made her happy, and Susan loved him too. Her life was now complete.

Jake Barton's life was far from complete. He hated every minute of his waking hours. The only time life was tolerable was when he was asleep, and that wasn't easy inside a prison. When the lights were out at night, the noise began. The incarcerated men made their feelings felt once they were in the dark. Some yelled and cursed, others groaned in their sleep. Others held arguments and shouted insults through the locked doors. Some nights it was just mayhem. The only way Jake could sleep was with his pillow over his head, which didn't improve his temper, and one day, outside, during the exercise period, he found one of the prisoners on his block who'd often ruined his sleep and attacked him.

The other prisoners surrounded the two men, forming a circle, cheering them on, excited by the fight, yelling encouragement at both men. 'Kick him! Kill him!' It was the best entertainment they'd had for a long time.

Eventually, the two men were separated by several warders armed with truncheons and marched away to see the governor. Both were bruised and bleeding from their encounter.

Jake was first to face the governor. His lip was bleeding, his eyes were beginning to swell, his prison clothes were torn. But his anger had far from abated. He glared at the man seated at the desk, who was looking at him.

'You can take that look off your face, Barton,' the governor said. 'Your temper won't get you anywhere in here! Now perhaps you'll be good enough to explain to me what happened to cause such behaviour on your part, because I'm told you started this fracas.'

'That bastard keeps me awake every night with his yelling. No matter how many times he's told to shut up he carries on. Well, I'd had enough!'

'I can understand how difficult this can be, Barton, but I'm afraid it's part of prison life. You just have to suck your teeth and get on with it.'

'You wouldn't if you were in my place!'

'But I wouldn't be in your place! You are here, Barton, because you broke the law! Life in prison isn't meant to be a bowl of cherries. You are here to serve time for a crime. It isn't meant to be comfortable. For the next month your exercise will only be for thirty minutes, and it will be on your own.' He nodded to the warder. 'Take him to the nurse to be cleaned up!'

Inside the prison hospital, the nurse attended to his wounds while a warden who'd taken him there stood by. He flinched as she bathed the cuts on his lip and his eye.

'Keep still, Mr Barton, don't be a baby!'

He muttered beneath his breath. But as

she worked, he gazed around. He was in a side room, and through the open door he saw the ward with several empty beds lined up and beyond – and two that had patients in them.

'What happened to them?' he asked.

'One has a broken leg from falling down the stairs, and the other's had an operation for appendicitis.'

Lucky devils, he thought. The ward was clean and spacious, unlike his cell which was claustrophobic. Although the main door was locked and a warden sat on duty, there was a feeling of freedom and peace here, and Jake longed to climb into a comfortable bed. Here he could get a good night's sleep. The thought nagged at him as he was led back to his cell.

His mood didn't improve when at lunchtime he lined up with the other prisoners for his meal and sat down at a table. The man next to him was reading a local paper, and Jake saw an article about Sam Knight. Barton asked to look at it.

Knight had been interviewed and there was a picture of him standing in front of his new premises with a racing car and a well-known driver. Sam had told the reporter he'd retired from the racetrack and was now working on racing cars for other drivers – and that business was brisk.

Barton's heart sank. Without Sam Knight

racing against him, Jake was aware that he could have shone, could have more than likely been a winner. He would have been the one holding the trophies, not Knight. But what chance had he now? Yet again Sam Knight was courting success, whilst he was rotting away in prison!

Sam and his boys were working on a car that was to be driven in the next twenty-four-hour race at Le Mans. It was the most important job he'd been given, and he was thrilled. The driver was internationally famous, and Sam knew if the man did well in the race, he'd be made. He had another month to complete the engine he'd built especially for the vehicle.

It was during this time that there was a riot at the prison. Prisoners had taken over a block inside and were holding several warders as hostages, and it was rumoured that a couple of prisoners had escaped. The papers were full of it, as was the radio and television.

RIOTS AT LEWES PRISON. WARDERS HELD AS HOSTAGES. Those were the headlines in the local paper.

Inside the prison it was mayhem. Guns were issued to the prison warders, who donned padded body armour in readiness. The governor was giving his orders, but the prisoners were relentless, threatening to kill the warders if anyone tried to enter the block. They had demands – better food and more time with their families on visiting days were but a few of them.

Fires were started in some of the cells, furniture was broken. Beds were overturned and bedding shredded.

During this time Jake Barton and another prisoner had taken the keys off one of the warders and made their way to another room, where they managed to climb through a shaft which eventually led them on to a roof overlooking the entrance to the prison. It was getting dark, and below them was a large van which had brought in clean linen. The driver and his mate had unloaded the van and were inside the office, where they were told to drive out whilst they could do so safely.

Jake felt this was his only chance, and he jumped on to the top of the van just before the two men walked out and climbed into the vehicle. The other prisoner was too late to do so. He saw Jake lying flat on the roof, hanging on to a bar which ran either side of the roof as the van drove out of the gates to freedom.

Twenty-Four

In the gathering dusk, Jake clung on to the bars as he lay on the roof of the van, keeping flat so as not to be seen. The vehicle eventually pulled into the yard of the laundry, turned and parked up against a wall. It was quiet as by now the occupants of the main building had finished work for the day. The two men climbed out of the vehicle, locked it and walked out of the main gate. Barton was alone.

He quietly sat up, flexing his fingers, which were stiff, having gripped the rail hard during the journey. Barton looked around. The laundry was in darkness. Other delivery vans were parked alongside his. To the left was a small building, also in darkness. Barton climbed down and stretched. He was free! He was bloody well free!

He walked over to the smaller building and peered through the window. He could just make out several brown overalls hanging up against one wall. He wanted one to cover his prison uniform before he dare walk on to the street. He tried the door but it was locked. He walked to the side and saw a window, which was closed. His eyes narrowed as he collected his thoughts. Then he peered round the building looking at the street for passers-by, but everything was quiet. Removing one shoe, he smashed the window and waited. There wasn't a sound to be heard. He removed the broken glass from the frame and hoisted himself over the sill. Once inside, he took out his lighter, flicked back the top and lit it. Then he found an overall that fitted and put it on.

He rummaged around the place, pocketing various things he thought might be of use and happened upon a piece of equipment that was just what he needed for the plan he had in mind. Then, climbing back out of the window, he walked out of the gate.

Sam and Connie were dining at their favourite restaurant at the Cowherds Inn. Sam was telling her how pleased he was with his work in progress.

'The engine is so sweet,' he said. 'She seems to purr when you start her up.'

'Her?' Connie chuckled. 'It's a she? The way you talk about her makes me quite jealous!'

He was highly amused. 'And so you should be! She does whatever I want. She purrs when I switch her on, and when I press my foot on the accelerator she roars into life, which excites me. I love the sound of her voice.'

'But she can't do the things that I can to excite you, darling. And ... you can't cuddle up to her in bed, feel her warm body against yours!'

Laughing, he said, 'There you do have a point.' He reached across the table and took her hand. 'Things are going really well now, sweetheart. Business is brisk, our future is now secure. I think it's time for us to make our own plans.'

Her breath caught in her throat. 'What are you saying, Sam?'

'I'm saying, will you marry me?'

How long she had waited to hear these words, yet when she did, she was taken aback. 'Marriage?'

'Yes, you silly woman. Marriage.' He grinned broadly at her. 'Unless you just want us to live together ... in sin, as your grandmother would put it.'

'I'd rather not,' she said quickly. 'You have no idea the comments I get about that. It would be worth getting married just to shut her up.'

'I was hoping you'd say yes because you loved me and couldn't live without me!' But his mouth twitched at the corners as he spoke.

'I do want to marry you, Sam Knight, and it *is* because I love you and can't live without you.'

'That's a yes then?'

'Most definitely!'

He raised her hand to his lips and kissed it. 'That's wonderful. Tomorrow we'll go and buy you a ring, then you can flash that in front of Madge's eyes. Now let's have a glass of champagne to celebrate.'

Later, as they left the restaurant, Sam said, 'If you don't mind I want to call into the garage. I left some papers there which I need for the morning to take to the bank. Do you mind? It won't take a minute.'

'No, of course not.'

They climbed into the car and drove away.

When they arrived at their destination, Sam said, 'You stay there, I won't be long.'

Connie didn't object. She wanted to be alone to digest the fact that she was now officially engaged to the man she adored – and had so nearly lost.

Sam took out his keys to the garage as he walked up to the door. He went to unlock the padlock when he noticed the chain which held the doors together with the lock had been cut. Putting the keys into his pocket, he opened the door slowly and quietly. He was shocked at the scene before him as he crept inside.

Jake Barton was holding a can of petrol and pouring the contents over the racing car that Sam had been working on, unaware that in his frenzy he was splashing the fuel on himself too. Sam realized the danger they were in.

'What the bloody hell do you think you're doing, Barton?'

Jake, shaken by the sudden voice, stopped and turned.

When he saw Sam standing there, he put down the can, took his lighter out of his pocket, flicked the top back and, lighting it, held it high.

'Don't come any closer, you bastard!' His laugh had the sound of hysteria in it.

'Don't be a fool!' said Sam, quietly. 'You'll blow us both to kingdom come.'

'What do I care, Knight? No way am I going to stay locked up for another two years in that hellhole! You have no idea what it's like. There's no way I'm going back inside, so I've come to settle a score.'

'I wasn't aware we had anything to settle,' said Sam, trying to calm him.

Jake glared at him with unconcealed hatred. 'You have been a thorn in my side ever since you started racing. But for you I too could have made a name for myself, been the local hero, but no, it was always you. I am a better driver than you any day.'

'You might be right,' said Sam. 'If you had concentrated on the race instead of me, you might have been the one to stand on the podium with the trophy. But you were full of hate and spite.' He paused. 'It could have

292

been so different, Barton. We could have been friends.'

'Ha! Never! Now you're set to make a mint and I'm here to stop you. Once this car is destroyed no one will give you the time of day. If you can't keep their precious vehicles safe, they won't want to trust you again.'

Outside, Connie was getting restless. What on earth was keeping Sam? He'd said he would only be a minute. She got out of the car. As she walked to the door she heard voices and frowned. As she was about to walk in, she heard the voice of Jake Barton threatening Sam. She pushed the door open and when she saw what was happening and realized the danger her Sam was in she screamed.

Taken by surprise, Jake's attention was distracted, and Sam took advantage of it. Leaping forward he grabbed Barton by his clothes and drew him away from the car, throwing him towards the door. The lighter fell from Barton's fingers on to his petrol soaked clothes, which ignited. He screamed as the flames touched his flesh.

Sam dived for the fire extinguisher that was by the door and covered the blazing figure with foam.

'Ring for an ambulance and the police!' he yelled to Connie.

She was so shocked she just stared at him. 'Now!'

It was enough to get her moving and she ran towards the phone.

Sam then sprayed the car and surround with foam just in case it too caught fire, and then he turned his attention to Jake Barton. As he knelt beside him, he was appalled at the sight. Barton's face was blistered, his hands burnt, his clothes scorched to ashes, showing the injured flesh beneath. Quietly Sam said, 'You bloody fool, Jake.'

The ambulance arrived within minutes. 'Jesus!' exclaimed the driver when he saw Barton. 'What happened here?'

Sam quickly explained as they gingerly lifted Jake, who was moaning in pain, on to a stretcher. They then rushed him to the hospital.

Connie was trembling as Sam held her. 'It's all right, darling.'

'Oh Sam, I thought he was going to set the garage alight. I thought I was going to lose you.' She burst into tears just as the police arrived.

When Sam explained what had happened, he was asked how Barton could have gained entry, but as they searched the premises they discovered a pair of steel cutters.

'God knows where he found these,' Sam remarked. 'They aren't mine.'

They drove to the police station so that Sam and Connie could make statements.

When he'd finished, Sam asked the officer if there had been any news from the hospital.

'No, sir, not yet. We'll let you know if we hear. Now I suggest you take the young lady home, she's still in shock.'

Once they were inside the flat, Sam made Connie a cup of tea with sugar and brandy in it, then, sitting beside her on the settee, he insisted she drank it. He kept an arm around her and a blanket over her knees, as she still was trembling.

As she sipped her tea, Sam talked to her. 'Well, that was quite a night. First I propose to my girl and then nearly lose everything!'

'Why does that man hate you so?'

'I really have no idea. When we began racing against each other, I won the first two races. After that Jake saw me as his rival, but he couldn't stand being beaten, especially by me. There's no rhyme or reason to it, sadly.'

'Do you think he'll recover?' She was almost afraid to ask.

Sam shook his head. 'I really don't know, he was so very badly burnt. If he recovers he'll have to endure many operations, and skin grafting, like they did with the airmen in the war. It doesn't bear thinking about.' He paused. 'There was a sort of madness about him tonight. He said he couldn't go back to prison, said it was a hellhole. The whole thing could have been avoided, that's the saddest thing of all. Three men with ruined lives, all for money.'

At that moment the telephone rang and Sam got up to answer it. 'Yes, speaking.' He listened, then said, 'Thank you for letting me know.'

He walked back to Connie, sat down and held her. 'That was the police. Jake Barton just passed away. I can't help thinking that in his case it was for the best; he was so badly injured. There will be an inquest later, of course.'

She looked at him with apprehension. 'Will we have to go?'

'I'm afraid so. We'll have to give evidence so that they can deliver a verdict.' He looked at Connie. 'Come on, darling, let's go to bed. I don't know about you but I'm worn out, physically and mentally.'

The following morning, Tom and Harry arrived to work as usual only to find Sam cleaning the car. The smell of petrol filled the air.

'What the hell is going on?' asked Tom.

The two men were shocked when Sam relayed the events of the previous night.

'Bloody hell!' Harry exclaimed. 'You were lucky, mate. The whole place could have blown up!'

'Jake Barton wasn't so lucky. He died last night.'

The men were shocked at the news. 'What an idiot,' said Tom. 'He wasted his talent, all for nothing. Still, I'm sorry to hear he died in such a way.'

'Me too,' Sam agreed. 'However, we still have a business to run, so let's get on with it.'

Two weeks later, the inquest took place. Both Sam and Connie gave their evidence and a verdict of 'death by misadventure' was brought in. They both left the court with a feeling of sadness. It had been an ordeal for all concerned.

Meantime the prison riot had been quelled; the other missing prisoner had given himself up, having lost the opportunity to escape. But the gossip inside for days to follow was of Jake Barton's horrific death. It cast a feeling of gloom around the prison.

In mid August the wedding of Connie and Sam took place at St Mark's Church. It was a beautiful day and there were crowds gathered watching, mainly fans of the popular driver. The press were out in force, light bulbs flashing as the groom arrived with his two best men. Tom and Harry had both insisted on the role!

Both families took their place in church. Madge resplendent in lilac and smiling and posing for the cameras. Enjoying the fact that her granddaughter was marrying someone so famous in her home town.

There were cheers when Connie arrived with her father. As the car pulled up in front of the church, her proud father, seeing the crowd, asked, 'Are you ready, love?'

'Oh yes, Dad. This is the happiest day of my life, and I'm going to enjoy every moment!'

Her friend Betty, her only bridesmaid, dressed in pale pink, was waiting. She grinned broadly at Connie. 'You look smashing!' she said.

Connie's wedding dress was ivory, her bouquet cream and tea coloured roses, her veil held in place with a jewelled headdress.

Betty fussed about her, straightening the train until they were ready. And the bridal party entered the church.

The organ started, the congregation stood and the service began.

The reception was held at the Polygon Hotel. As Connie stood with her husband, greeting her guests, she thought it ironic that both she and John's ex-wife had celebrated their new lives at the same place. It didn't detract from her enjoyment, it seemed fitting in a strange way, and she couldn't help but think that the games lovers played never quite worked out to plan.

After the reception, the bride and groom eventually made their way to a room they'd booked to change out of their finery and into clothes fit for travel.

As Connie slipped out of her wedding dress, Sam drew her into his arms and kissed her.

'Well, Mrs Knight, this has been a lovely day. A good beginning to a great life together. We are going to have so much fun.'

She gazed into his eyes. 'I can hardly wait,' she said.

Sam nuzzled her neck. 'You don't have to; we have time before we have to leave the hotel.' He picked her up and carried her to the bed.

As they lay together, Connie said, 'Let's get a few things sorted first.'

He looked surprised. 'Like what?'

'Just to let you know I expect you to bring me a cup of tea in bed every morning before I get up and cook the breakfast,' she said, teasing him.

He started laughing. 'Trying to lay the law down already, are you? Well, Mrs Knight, I'm the one who wears the trousers in this marriage!'

'All men think that. You have a lot to learn about women, darling,' she said, 'but I'm going to have the time of my life teaching you!'

But as she gazed into the eyes of her groom, she knew they would both learn from each other in the many years ahead.

The publishers hope that this book has given you enjoyable reading. Large Print Books are especially designed to be as easy to see and hold as possible. If you wish a complete list of our books please ask at your local library or write directly to:

Magna Large Print Books
Magna House, Long Preston,
Skipton, North Yorkshire.
BD23 4ND

This Large Print Book, for people
who cannot read normal print,
is published under the auspices of

THE ULVERSCROFT FOUNDATION